Howls and Hallows

THE RED CAPE SOCIETY, BOOK 5

MELANIE KARSAK

CLOCKPUNK PRESS

Howls and Hallows
A Red Riding Hood Retelling
The Red Cape Society, Book 5
Copyright © 2018 Clockpunk Press
All rights reserved. No part of this book may be used or reproduced without permission from the author.
This is a work of fiction. References to historical people, organizations, events, places, and establishments are the product of the author's imagination or are used fictitiously. Any resemblance to living persons is purely coincidental.
Published by Clockpunk Press
Editing by Becky Stephens Editing
Proofreading by Siren Editing
Cover art by Art by Karri

❦ Created with Vellum

for my ARC Team…
Thank you, thank you, thank you

Howls and Hallows

CHAPTER 1
Back in Red

I banked the steambike left, making the tight turn. Keeping one eye on the row of buildings beside me, I watched as the werewolf jumped from rooftop to rooftop. The wolf looked down at me, his red eyes glaring with hatred.

Wolves.

I pressed the accelerator. The wolf was running out of rooftops, and I was running out of road, as we both raced toward the Thames. I knew bloody well that he had a ship waiting for him. One of us was going to get there first. Which one, I wasn't yet sure.

Focusing my attention back on the narrow cobblestone street, I weaved around horse carts, autos, and irritated pedestrians. The fog was dense, the orange glow of the gaslamps barely cutting through the mist. Master Hart had configured me a new pair of goggles.

The optics enhanced the shadows detected by my mooneye. As I raced toward the river, an ethereal sailor floated past. It was just days before All Hallows. The entire city was alive with…well, the undead. The dark district, wild on a regular day, was like a preternatural circus. With the city brimming with the supernatural, how had I ended up chasing jewel thieves?

I'd been chasing this rogue pack of wolves all autumn. They were crafty little mutts, five in all in their crew. They'd started their shenanigans in Rome, moved to Venice, then hit Paris, and now they were here. Pilfering banks, museums, and stately homes, the thieves were remarkably good compared to the usual blundering of werewolves. Given they were not a local problem, Sir Blackwood decided to let them be an issue for the Red Cape Society to handle. I almost argued. Almost. But things had been decidedly neutral between Sir Blackwood and me, and I wanted to keep it that way since there was no telling when—or if—Lionheart ever planned to return, an issue that dogged my mind much to my extreme annoyance. With the Templars out of the picture, it was up to the Red Capes to take out this cell of bandits. Where my colleagues abroad had failed, I would succeed. The reputation of the Red Capes depended on it. And I wasn't about to let the realm down.

Ahead, I spotted the dark waters of the Thames. The

waves slapped along the breakers. Slowing the bike, I turned the machine, skidding sideways to a stop. I quickly jumped off, my red cape billowing behind me. I rushed to the end of the row then cast a glance out at the water. Just offshore, I spotted a small boat. The vessel was perfectly positioned so that anyone with extraordinary, preternatural strength could leap from the rooftop at the edge of the wharf onto the ship.

I smirked. My plan was working.

Pulling both my pistols, I turned and waited.

Inhale.

Exhale.

The werewolf appeared at the edge of the roof.

I closed my right eye, looking out with my mooneye. Through my altered vision, I saw the wolf and the man all at once.

The wolf raised his maw, the light of the moon behind him making him glow, and let out a loud howl in celebration of his victory.

"Too soon, my friend, too soon," I whispered then pulled the trigger.

The werewolf's yowl halted with a wounded yip.

A moment later, there was a fiery explosion as the boat lingering offshore blasted apart in a fiery display.

The werewolf's body dropped from the rooftop. Holstering my pistols, I rushed to him. The werewolf—Yuri, the alpha of this thieving pack—was shifting back into human form. He tried to get up, but his leg failed him. My shots had been true but not lethal, as intended. The wolf fell to his knees. Cursing in Romanian, he glared at me. Pressing one hand against his stomach where blood seeped out, another on his lower leg, he spat at me when I came close.

"Now, Yuri. That's just rude. I could have killed you."

Lying not far away from him was a tattered satchel. I snatched the bag off the ground and opened it. Inside, I found a velvet box. I opened the lid. The circle of diamonds, on loan from Her Majesty for the express purpose of this set-up—and with many threats to send me on an expedition to Antarctica to hunt snow monsters if I let the assailants get away with her crown jewels—was safe within.

I looked over my shoulder toward the Thames. Fast moving ships—Red Capes—were already closing in on the wreckage. I chuckled seeing the wolves dog-paddling toward shore as if their lives depended on it. But there was no escaping. They were surrounded.

I caught movement out of the corner of my eye as someone approached us. Turning, I found Agent Harper making her way toward me, a device in hand.

"Got it?" she asked.

I nodded, looking down at the diamond necklace. "Suppose she'll let me keep it in reward?"

Harper laughed. "Not likely."

Yuri, who was still cursing at me, turned his venom toward Harper.

Harper frowned at him. "Don't be ungrateful. She could have killed you."

"That's what I told him."

"See my fireworks?" Harper asked, waggling the detonator in her hand.

"So I did. Well done, *Senior* Agent Harper."

"Well, I wanted to close my first official case as your partner with a bang."

Good-naturedly, I rolled my eyes at her. "I thought we covered this already. No puns."

"Sorry. Appears I picked up some bad habits in the field."

"We'll have you right in no time," I said then looked down at Yuri. "I'd cuff you, but you'd probably bleed to death," I said then lifted the werewolf off the ground, hauling him toward the dock where an agency boat would collect him. "Don't worry, Yuri. We'll have you all nice and healed up in time for prison," I said then turned back to Harper. "And the other goods?"

"Got word half an hour ago. Agent Fox locked down the wolves on guard and secured the airship and its treasures."

I grinned at Harper. She'd returned from abroad just after the case with Alodie, and Edwin had formally assigned her as my partner. Thankfully, save these thieving devils, it had been relatively quiet. But all the same, I was glad she was back. Nothing stays quiet for long.

"Why are you grinning at me like that?" Harper asked.

"I think I might have missed you, Harper."

"I might have missed you too, Louvel."

Yuri swore at us both—decidedly not interested in our mutual respect—making us both laugh.

CHAPTER 2
Every Eligible Maiden

With the wolves safely locked down, Harper and I headed back to headquarters to check in and, of course, do paperwork. Not that I minded. I knew Edwin would be there. I was surprised, however, to find him lingering by my desk when we arrived.

He smiled when he saw me—that soft, shy smile he reserved for me alone.

My whole body felt warmed by the glow. In truth, things had been a little strained after the case with Alodie. Edwin was perceptive, and he had seen whatever that something was between Lionheart and me. But he had never questioned me. It was an honor I wasn't entirely sure I deserved.

With Lionheart gone, I was able to set that odd moment aside. I hardly ever thought about it—at least, that's the mantra I told myself. Everything went back to normal. Edwin and I carried forward. Nothing changed except my move to Vesta's Grotto, as Grand-mère insisted we call our new home. On that topic, I might have smudged the truth from Edwin a little. *A gift from the Templars*—that's what I'd told him. Which Templar, I didn't specify. He didn't ask. I didn't divulge. But I felt a healthy amount of guilt over it. Yet what was I supposed to do? Keeping my grand-mère safe outweighed everything, and Lionheart had literally given me the key to making that happen. Despite my feelings for Edwin, or the strangeness between Lionheart and me, there was one person to whom I was beholden: Grand-mère. Those were the facts of the matter. What I felt about what had happened between Lionheart and me was far more confusing. But he'd left, so I was pretty much on my own when it came to figuring out what that kiss was all about. With Lionheart missing, it made it a lot easier to pretend nothing had happened. It made it a lot easier to forget. Kind of.

As Harper and I approached, I noticed that Edwin was holding a leather binder.

"New brief," Harper said.

I nodded. I wasn't surprised that something new was going wrong, but I wasn't thrilled either. Jessica was due within the next couple of weeks, and I was anticipating becoming an unofficial aunt to baby Briarwood. I had hoped things would stay quiet enough that I'd have time to go fuss over the baby when the time came. No chance of getting that lucky.

"I see you mean to keep us busy," I told Edwin as I eyed the folder.

"I wanted to make sure Agent Harper was properly broken in to her new post."

"Properly broken in?" Harper exclaimed in mock protest. "You did read my report from the field, didn't you?"

"That I did," Agent Hunter said then grinned. "You forgot to file Form 1101."

Harper laughed. "Well, dock it from my pay."

Edwin grinned good-naturedly at her then turned to me. "I did have an inquiry from Her Majesty."

I pulled the velvet box from the bag. "Her Majesty's baubles are secure." I handed the box to Edwin, suppressing a sigh when I did so. I would have liked to try it on, just once, just for the hell of it.

Edwin chuckled lightly and took the box from my hand. "Shall we?" he asked, motioning to his office.

We crossed the workroom. It was almost dawn, but many other agents were already at their desks. This time of year was always busy for the Red Cape Society. Nothing like the lead-up to All Hallows to get all the preternaturals riled up. I waved to Hank and Cressida who were busy bickering over something. They paused their argument long enough to acknowledge Harper and me then went back fighting. I eyed the place for Agent Rose, but there was no sign of her. I also scanned for Agent Ewan Goodwin—a Pellinore whose case I worked on over the summer—but he wasn't there either. No doubt he was at Willowbrook Park. Edwin had loaned his family home to the society for use by the Pellinores. I hadn't broken the news to Grand-mère yet that her vision of a fine country estate was off the chessboard.

Harper and I followed Edwin into his office then took our seats opposite his at his desk. He handed the brief to Harper.

"When I was at Eaton, I made the acquaintance of Lord Edison Cabell," Edwin began. "He is a good friend, and his family holds an annual All Hallows Ball at his estate in the Fenlands. It's attended by many notable peers and is the highlight of the autumn season. His family, however, is cursed. The setting and the curse evoke a delightfully eerie milieu for people who would be quite scandalized to know their play at the macabre touches very close to the truth of our realm. Regardless, Edison wrote to me about some strange happenings at the estate. He is aware that I worked with the peculiar and asked for my help," Edwin explained as Harper leafed through the brief.

"You're sending us?" I asked.

Edwin nodded. "I wanted to send my best agents."

I raised a playful eyebrow at him.

Edwin smiled.

"You said the Cabells are cursed. What exactly are they cursed with?" Harper asked.

She pulled a sketch of the manor house from the folder and handed it to me. The Gothic style mansion screamed old money and bad vibes. "Or *who* are they cursed *by*?" I added.

Harper nodded to me.

"On the lands lorded over by the Cabells there was once a small settlement that was home to a coven—or so the legend says. Back in the sixteenth century, Lord Bran Cabell rounded up the local witches and burned them at the stake. With their dying breath, the witches cursed the family. Any heir who steps foot on holy ground— the coven site—will die in a fortnight. Lord Bran himself was found dead at the location of the coven shortly after the burning."

"Sounds like he deserved it," I said.

"Found dead. Dead how?" Harper asked.

"Lord Bran was found with his throat ripped out," Edwin replied.

"Well, that would do it," I said.

Harper rolled her eyes at me.

"The descendants of Lord Bran Cabell have always been careful to avoid the site. But Edison has always been interested in the family curse, interested in learning if there is any truth behind it. He once expressed an interest in finding a way to making reparations. Edison recently visited the ruins. Three nights later, something came howling at Cabell Manor."

Now I understood why Edwin had asked Harper and me to work the case.

"Werewolves?" Harper asked. "A werewolf curse? What's the connection with the witches though. I don't get it."

"Werewolves, hellhounds, banshee. God only knows what it might be. But between the howling and the throat ripping…" Edwin said.

I nodded. "A werewolf could live for centuries, carrying on a curse. And a wolf could survive burning at the stake."

"Nasty business," Harper said. "So, the fens?" she asked, turning to me.

"A country job. Shall we get rustic?" I asked Agent Harper.

"Country, yes. Rustic, no," Edwin said, motioning to the drawing of the manor I was holding. "The Cabells are very wealthy and have a prominent place in good society."

"The Cabells. Is Lord Cabell married?" Harper asked.

Edwin shifted slightly, lacing then unlacing his

fingers. His nervous movement didn't escape my notice. "No. Lord Cabell and his sister, Lady Charlotte, live at Cabell Manor."

"Lady Charlotte," Harper whispered, making a note in the brief.

I tried to meet Edwin's eyes, but he kept his gaze on Harper.

Curiouser and curiouser.

"I'm afraid the whole affair is very ill-timed. Since the All Hallows Ball is this week, Edison was anxious to get this matter settled," Edwin said.

"Ah, so they're hoping we'll have this mess cleaned up before the party. How posh," I said with a roll of the eyes.

"Having actual monsters at an All Hallows Ball would upset Lady Charlotte's carefully organized event," Edwin said then chuckled to himself.

I tried not to frown. Whoever Lady Charlotte was, I didn't like her already.

"Once I finish up some work here, I'll join you at Cabell Manor," Edwin said.

"The curse," Harper said with a shake of the head as she flipped through the brief. "Something feels missing here. I'll check our records. I want to do a search for any information we might have on the coven."

Feeling annoyed with Edwin, the posh Lord Cabell, and whomever this tart Lady Charlotte was, I rose.

"Good idea. Why don't I join you? There is some info in our files about some stray wolves who left the city a few centuries back. Vagabonds, really. We never had any trouble with them, so no one ever followed up. Let me see where they went."

"Clem—Agent Louvel, may I have a moment first?" Edwin asked.

Agent Harper rose and went to the door. "I'll go get started. Join me when you're done?"

I nodded.

With a wave, Harper left Edwin and me alone.

Sucking in my petty jealousies, I turned back to Edwin. Who was I to be jealous of—well, I didn't even know what. A smile? An avoided glance? Who was I to worry about Edwin's past, especially when I hadn't stopped thinking about Lionheart every other moment since he'd left?

"I'm sorry to send you out of the city," Edwin said. He rose and came around the desk to join me.

"I'm sorry to go."

"I'm sure the Templars will keep things quiet while you're gone."

I nodded. "I'll send word to Sir Blackwood."

Edwin laced his fingers behind his back then coughed lightly. "Any news of Sir Richard?"

I felt like a rock dropped into the pit of my stomach. "No."

"Clemeny, I... I wanted to ask something."

Oh. No. This can't be good. "Of course."

"I generally attend the All Hallows Ball as a guest. I'm invited this year as well. I was hoping, assuming the case doesn't get out of hand and spoil the event, that you would stay on and attend as my date."

"Your date. For a ball?"

"Yes," he said.

"I... Of course." *Oh, thank god.*

Edwin smiled happily, his hands relaxing to his sides once more. "I'm sorry to force you to armor up *and* procure a ballgown."

I chuckled. "It's all right. A true lady should be ready for both smiting and waltzing."

"Was there ever a more perfect woman?"

I grinned, flattered by the compliment but feeling that strange sting of guilt once more. Perfect women didn't go around kissing werewolves while they were attached to someone else. I was far from perfect. "Thank you, Edwin. I'm honored you asked."

Edwin smiled then set his fingers gently on my chin. "I'm honored you said yes."

Edwin leaned in and set a gentle kiss on my lips. I caught his delightful cinnamon scent. My heart pattered quickly, yearning for more. Edwin was still so measured, so careful. Maybe he was right to be so. Maybe my instincts were the ones that were off-kilter. It wouldn't be proper to just scoop someone up and press a passionate kiss on their lips. Right?

When Edwin stepped back, he smiled gently at me, his blue eyes meeting mine.

"I don't know what you're going to find out there. Something has Edison rattled. Be careful."

I blew air through my lips. "Nothing to worry about. I have Harper now."

Edwin chuckled.

"You could tell Victoria I'm going to a ball. That necklace would look very nice with my gown," I said.

Edwin tapped the box sitting on his desk. "I'll mention it."

Passing Edwin a knowing wink, I turned and headed to join Harper.

CHAPTER 3
Vesta's Grotto

After a thorough check of the Agency's records, I set off back across town to the grotto. It was just after dawn when I arrived. Unlocking the gate, I walked the steambike inside. I'd grown accustomed to driving the bike after Lionheart left. When he returned, he'd have a hard time getting it back.

If he came back.

When he came back.

Beams of early morning sunlight filtered through the trees and down onto Grand-mère who was working in the garden. I smiled at the sight. It had taken some doing, including a few well-contrived lies, to convince Grand-mère to leave her flat and move here. I had somehow managed to make her believe I had saved up enough money to buy the place, and that through my agency connections, I'd found a place on holy ground where we could be together and safe.

It was clear to me that Grand-mère did not entirely believe my story, but when she saw the little house, and its pretty garden, she decided not to pay attention to her nagging suspicions, much to my relief.

Twisting the truth to Edwin had felt harder. Edwin trusted me. If there was something to tell, he trusted me to say it. But there was nothing to tell. Not really. Lionheart was broken by Bryony's death, that was all. That night, Lionheart had been confused, not himself. The house was just a gift. That's all. When Lionheart came back—if he came back—everything would go back to normal. Everything would be fine. Next time, I would do a better job at keeping my distance.

When he came back.

If he came back.

When was he coming back, exactly?

I smothered the confused feelings that started bubbling up. I could already feel my face contorting into weird and ugly shapes. I didn't want Grand-mère asking questions I couldn't answer. Shaking the thoughts of that smirking werewolf from my mind, I crossed the lawn toward her.

"Look, my Clemeny, how pretty my chrysanthemums are," she said, gently touching the rust-colored blossom with the tips of her fingers. "But the rest of the flowers are fading," she said with a sigh. She rose, clapping the dirt off her hands onto her apron.

"The whole garden is beautiful, Grand-mère."

"It will be, in the spring. Now the earth is going to sleep. Look at those colors," she said, pointing to the oak growing along the wall of the garden. The leaves on the tree had turned a vibrant orange color.

I looked up at the leaves, feeling the sunlight on my face. A brisk wind whipped across the lawn. Winter was coming.

"By next summer, I'll have this garden full of blossoms and smelling like a perfumery. Let's go inside. You'll be hungry. And how was your evening?"

"I saved the crown jewels."

Grand-mère laughed. "Oh, my Clemeny. Of course, you did. Of course."

I set my hands on my hips. "You know, Grand-mère, I really did."

She chuckled. "I'm sure the Queen will be very grateful. Now, let's go inside," she said, taking my arm and leading me toward the small house. "I have been going through the attic. Such a mess. But there are some interesting books up there, church records left behind. I'm going to clean everything up, catalog them properly. And on the old Roman wall, I found some strange markings. This house is such a treasure."

"I'm glad you're happy here, Grand-mère."

"Such a good find. So peaceful. So quiet. My good girl, how did you find this house again?"

"Through the agency."

"But how?"

"Someone knew about the place."

"Yes, but who?"

"I forget. I do have some news you're going to want to hear," I said, trying desperately to change the subject.

"And that is?"

"I've been invited to a ball."

Grand-mère gasped. "A ball? Where? At Willowbrook Park?"

I grinned. "No, Grand-mère. Another place in the country. But Edwin invited me to be his date."

"Oh, my Clemeny! Oranges and lemons. Very good. Such a fine man. Maybe he'll propose."

"Let's not be hasty."

"You never know, my girl. Sir Edwin is certainly sweet on you."

My cheeks burned red. "How did Grand-père propose to you?"

Grand-mère laughed. "In an apple orchard. He bent to propose to me, and a bee stung his knee. He didn't tell me. He proposed to me with tears streaming down his cheeks. I was so moved by his emotion, I said yes. Only afterward did he tell me about the bee."

We both laughed.

"No, no, a ball will do very well. No more apple orchards. Love can sting sometimes," she said with a chuckle.

Love can sting sometimes.

My insides felt like they were melting. I could feel the blood leaching from my face. Good god, what if Edwin did propose?

Grand-mère pinched my cheek. "Peaky. You need breakfast."

"Yes, I do. And lots of it."

Grand-mère chuckled. "I hope you'll be back in time to see Quinn's baby."

"Well, I'm pretty sure it's not going anywhere even if I miss the birth."

Grand-mère sighed with exasperation. "Even so, Quinn will need you there to pluck up his courage."

"Right. You're right."

"But Clemeny, a ball! How wonderful. But my dear, what will you wear? The blue dress was ruined by all that…goo."

"You mean Phillip Phillips."

Grand-mère clicked her tongue at me. "What? Nevermind. You do have that old green frock. You should take it just in case, but it's not suitable for a ball. Do you have time to get something?"

I cast a glance up at the window of my bedchamber. "Don't worry, Grand-mère. I have a dress."

Grand-mère sent me upstairs to freshen up while she rattled around the kitchen to make some breakfast. She was happily singing in French, no doubt imagining me like Cinderella at the ball.

Her words rattled around in my head. Edwin surely wasn't planning to propose, was he? I mean, that seemed rash. No. He just wanted me to meet his old friends in a social setting—even this Lady Charlotte. It would be good to see him in that world. I needed to see what he was really like.

I pulled off my armor, slipped on a robe, and went to my wardrobe. Pushing aside my everyday items, I snagged the garment hanging in the very back of the wardrobe. Hooking the hanger on the closet door, I unzipped the garment bag. Red silk blossomed out of the bag like a rose opening under the sun. I stared at the dress. Yes. This would be perfect for the ball.

Perfect.

Except...

Except this dress was for someone else.

No. It was just a gift. Just a dress. It didn't mean anything. Lionheart was just confused. Everything was going to be fine. None of that was going to matter once he got back, if he came back. I zipped the bag up. This dress would work just fine for the ball. It was the right fashion and color. And it wasn't like I had the time or money to run around the city hunting something else to wear.

I pulled a trunk down from the top of the wardrobe then laid the dress inside. I snagged my old green gown, laying it in as well. If I remembered right, it was torn on the hem and had a burn on the sleeve where I'd gotten too close to a candle. I'd have to keep that in mind. Shaking my head, I loaded the case with my trousers, corsets, tops, armor, and a few extra weapons. I closed the lid.

Weapons and dresses stowed, I was ready to go to the ball.

CHAPTER 4

Not Exactly a Pumpkin Carriage

I met Harper at the airship platform in the early afternoon.

"Have your ginger?" she asked.

"Well, you're here," I replied.

Harper rolled her eyes. "I thought you said no puns."

I winked at her. Harper and I handed our trunks to a crewman then boarded the airship. Harper went to talk to the captain, and I found a spot to settle in. It wasn't long thereafter that the agency airship, sporting its signature red balloon, lifted off. The airship headed northeast toward the Fenlands. A marshy place, efforts to tame the land, which sat below sea level, had been ongoing since the Roman invasion.

"My digging turned up a few things," Harper said,

settling in beside me. She flipped open her leather binder.

I glanced at the brief. My stomach rolled, reminding me that I really shouldn't read while I was in motion. I dipped into my pocket and pulled out a candied ginger.

Harper chuckled but said nothing.

"Well?" I asked between chews. I was suddenly missing my—well, Lionheart's—steambike. There had to be a more comfortable, less vomit-inducing, way to get around besides airship.

"All right. Well. The intel we have on the old ruins near Cabell Manor indicates that there is something out there, but I'm not sure it's witches. I found a record of an encounter between the Romans and druids back when the Romans were attempting to build a road through the Fens. The Roman records briefly describe a small, religious community deep in the bog. The Roman records are really vague, but they called the inhabitants druids, not witches."

Druids.

"And what happened to our druid friends?"

"There is no mention of the druids or their religious settlement again. The Roman road was built quite a distance away from the Cabell estate. Could be the Romans decided on a better path, so they never bothered with the druids again."

"Or the druids frightened them off."

"Maybe. But you know the Romans. If they were frightened, they'd just slaughter everyone."

"Easy way to get over a fear."

"Nice and bloody, just how the Romans liked things."

"So, nothing else?"

"No. Nothing. Nothing about the estate, the ruins, or the nearby village."

"We're really doing a poor job of keeping an eye on happenings outside London. I need to bring that to Edwin's attention. We need agents deeper out in the field. The records I found were just as vague. I found three reports on the beta pack that left London in 1666: one in 1673, another in 1792, and the last in 1814. Otherwise, nothing. But the wolves were in eastern England in 1814."

"It is possible that whomever the Cabells irked back in the sixteenth century and the druids the Romans encountered are one in the same."

"A lot of time between the Romans and the sixteenth century. If the Roman records are even accurate. I'm sure every weird thing the Romans saw they attributed to the druids."

"True," Harper said. "The fens are a dodgy place. Lots of ruins, forgotten roads, and even villages that have been half-swallowed by the groundwater. It's a good place to hide."

Harper's brief was open to the sketch of Cabell Manor.

"Why build such an elaborate house in the middle of a swamp?" I asked.

"Good hunting and lots of farmland once the fen is drained. The manor sits on a rise. Lord Cabell's family raised the land. Lord Edison Cabell's great-grandfather employed Archibald Boatswain in the construction of a steam-powered drainage station near the mansion. Edison Cabell has expanded the number of stations on the property."

"Nice place for an All Hallows ball," I said.

Harper chuckled. "I brought a dress just in case we have to stay on. You?"

"Yeah." *A dress. The dress.*

"I'm sure Edwin will want you to stay."

I grunted.

"Wow, that was very wolf-like. Lionheart is rubbing off on you."

Was he ever. "Very funny."

"What, you don't want to attend a society ball?"

"Not particularly."

"Not even with Edwin?"

"Can we change the subject please?"

"All right, all right. Any hunches about the case?" Harper asked, tapping the image of the mansion.

"Let's see...hellhounds, werewolves, ghosts, or

pissed off druids? Hard to say until we talk to Lord Cabell. But howling and wolves pair well."

"At least it's not mummies," Harper said with a shudder.

"Mummies?"

Harper nodded then shuddered once more.

"One of these days, you're going to have to tell what, exactly, you did on rotation."

"You're going to need something stronger than a ginger chew."

At that, I laughed then leaned back into my seat. I was really glad Harper was back.

CHAPTER 5
Cabell Manor

It took most of the afternoon for the agency airship to make its way to the Cabell estate. My life was so firmly entrenched in the city that I was surprised to see that the countryside was ablaze with autumn colors. The trees made a palette of deep oranges, vibrant yellows, and blazing reds. The meadows were dotted with goldenrods and purple asters. The loamy smell of the earth even reached us aloft. Farmers toiled in the fields, loading bundles of golden wheat shafts into wagons.

As we'd traveled, I also got a good look at the fens. A vast, marshy region not far from the eastern coast, the land was picturesque in its natural beauty. The sun glimmered sweetly on the pools of water below, making the entire place look as if someone had tossed handfuls of silver coins across the landscape. The ponds shimmered with silvery light. But also evident were signs of human intervention. Windmills dotted the land, the wind providing power to pump the water away in order to make the land suitable for farming. A few steam-powered stations, their stacks rising high in the sky, also interrupted the charming view. The fens were being tamed, the water pushed into narrow channels, rows of farmland carved out of the natural landscape.

The trip took most of the afternoon. The sun was setting when the gables of Cabell Manor came into view. A thick fog had rolled in, occluding the land below. Even the massive mansion was hidden by the fog. The spires on the roof, the only part of the house still visible, looked like bony fingers pointing toward the sky. On the highest pinnacle was a statue of the Archangel Michael.

The agency airship slowed as it made its descent toward the estate. As we carefully descended into the mist, the jagged, gothic design of the place came more clearly into view. Cabell Manor looked more like an abbey than a stately mansion. There was an eerie silence to the place. Only the sorrowful sound of the waterfowl calling across the moor and the soft hiss of the nearby steam station whose stack was nearly as high as the manor's highest peak marked the place.

"Like something out of an Edgar Allen Poe story,"

Harper said. "No wonder they hold the All Hallows Ball here. It's strange."

"What's strange?"

"How normal people play at being scared. If they only knew…"

"That there are things they really should be afraid of?"

Harper nodded.

"I guess that's where we come in. We protect them from the real terrors so they can play and enjoy the rush of false fear, so they can enjoy their lives blissfully unaware."

"Well, from the sound of it, whatever Lord Cabell woke up has something more serious in mind than play. I just hope we find it first."

I cast a glance out at the fog-drenched landscape.

"Me too, partner. Me too."

THE AIRSHIP SUNK INTO THE FOG. BELOW, I SPIED THE SOFT glow of a blue lantern intended to guide the airship in. The illustration of the manor didn't do it justice. It was enormous. And as we lowered toward the ground, I could see that the grounds surrounding the place were massive. Gargoyles sat on the corners and peaks of the house, their angry faces glaring into the mist. A winding road led from the entrance of the house back out into the countryside. Behind the house was a tiered garden. Statues of angels and saints dotted the place, appearing like apparitions in the mist. Everything was utterly silent save the sound of the windmill turning on a rise not far away. An airship crewman rang a bell to alert the house to our arrival.

"Allo-ho-ho," he called, scanning the ground. "Anyone about?"

After a few moments, I heard the front door of the house squeak, and a figure moved through the mist.

"Allo-ho-ho," the crewman called once more.

"We have you, sir," a masculine voice called from below. "Drop your ladder. We'll secure you."

I raised an eyebrow at Harper.

"As long as it's not mummies, I don't care what's down there," Harper said, shuddering once more. She headed toward the rope ladder. A crewman took our parcels and headed down behind Harper. Securing my satchel, I moved to join them.

"Do you like speculative fiction, Agent Louvel?" Captain Franz, the agency airship captain, called.

"Not particularly. I spend too much time living the real thing, I suppose."

The man chuckled. "That's right. That's right. There's a common theme in those stories. This is the part where the wagon or carriage driver—or the friendly airship captain—says something ominous just before the hero departs into an obviously disturbed place. I was doing my best to come up with something, but I'm no Horace Walpole."

I chuckled. "Time to start reading romance novels, Captain Franz. Maybe even a good detective story. Don't want your imagination to get away with you. Regardless, ominous message received. It does look bloody haunted, doesn't it?"

"That it does, Agent Louvel. Good luck, and be careful."

"Of course," I said with a wave then climbed down the ladder.

I was about halfway down the ladder when I caught the sound of a church bell. There was no sweet peal of "oranges and lemons" but a somber gong that echoed across the moor. I glanced around the mist-drenched landscape.

Oh yeah, this place is definitely haunted. Wonderful.

I moved quickly down the ladder, joining Harper who was already waiting below. The airship crewman wasted no time climbing back up the rope and out of sight, leaving Harper and me alone with a tall man in a top hat and a long coat.

The man eyed us both skeptically then bowed. "Agents, I'm Frances, the butler. Welcome to Cabell Manor."

CHAPTER 6
Lord Cabell and Lady Charlotte

A moment later, a footman arrived. With a nod to Harper and me, he took our cases and headed inside.

"This way, Agents," the butler said, waving for us to follow.

"Is it always this foggy?" Harper asked.

"No. Usually, it's worse," he replied with a soft chuckle.

I cast a glance above me. The magenta-colored light cast by the airship balloon faded as the ship ascended back into the clouds and away from the manor. Frances, the butler, led us up a flight of stairs into the grand house. We entered a beautiful foyer with polished wood floors, a winding wooden stairwell, a massive crystal chandelier, and what appeared to be a farm stand's worth of gourds, fall leaves, bundled shafts of wheat, and even pumpkins.

"Are those pumpkins?" Harper asked.

Frances nodded. "Lady Charlotte had them brought in, adopting the American fashion to celebrate All Hallows. This is nothing. You should see the ballroom. The staff and I will spend the next few days carving them all," he said with an exasperated roll of the eyes. "Now, if you'll come with me," he said, leading us to the parlor. The room was comfortable and richly appointed. Turkish rugs lined the floors. Antique vases and crystal bowls decorated the tables. Silk and velvet upholstered cherry furniture filled the cozy space. A fire snapped in the hearth, giving the room a cheery glow—and making all the silver, crystal, and other visible symbols of wealth and refinement shimmer.

"I'll let Lord Cabell know you've arrived," Frances said then left Harper and me alone.

"Blimey," Harper whispered, spinning around as she looked. "This is…a lot."

"What? Not quite like home?"

Harper laughed. "Nothing like home."

"What about your family, Harper? What do your parents do for a living? Do you have any siblings?" I suddenly felt embarrassed when I realized I knew very little about Harper's real life.

"My father is a bank clerk. Mum stays at home, but

she does do some seamstress work from time to time. Mostly she's busy with my sisters. There are five of us. I'm the eldest. You have any brothers or sisters?"

"Not that I know of."

"Not that you know of?"

"Orphan. The widow Louvel adopted me."

"I didn't know that."

"Now you do."

A moment later, the parlor door opened, and a man about Edwin's age entered. He was a tall, thin man with very wispy blond hair and a pointed nose. He smiled widely, his manner open and cheerful. He wore an elegant grey suit with a dark blue waistcoat. A woman about the same age entered just behind him. She was beautifully dressed, her gown a deep burnt orange color and trimmed with gold beads.

"Agents, welcome. Welcome. Thank you so much for coming," the man said, crossing the room to meet us. "I'm Lord Cabell," he said, giving me a short bow. His eyes briefly skirted across my face, taking in the scar and eye, but his gaze didn't linger.

"Agent Louvel," I said, inclining my head to him—I'd be damned if I was going to curtsey. "And this is Agent Harper."

"Lord Cabell," Harper said politely.

Lord Cabell turned to Harper. I saw him pause. He

smiled widely at her. "Agent Harper." His gaze lingered on Harper's face a moment longer.

Long enough to make Harper's pale cheeks tint red.

The woman behind him coughed lightly.

Lord Cabell looked away from Harper and turned back to me. "Pleased to meet you, Agents. This is my sister, Lady Charlotte," he said, extending his arm toward the woman by means of introduction.

When I turned my attention to her, finally getting a good look at Lady Charlotte, I was surprised to see such a strong resemblance between her and Lord Cabell. Like Lord Cabell, she was tall, thin, and had wispy blonde hair. But the features that made Lord Cabell appear rather gaunt made Lady Charlotte appear ethereal and delicate.

"Before you ask, yes, we are twins," she said, her voice tinged with exasperation. She rolled her eyes.

I wasn't going to ask. I bit the inside of my cheek and forced myself not to look at Harper.

While Lady Charlotte smiled, there was a sharp, assessing manner in her gaze. Her mouth and eyes contradicted one another. She looked Harper over from head to toe, then she turned to me. When her glance finally reached my face—she'd started from my feet—I saw her startled surprise. She stared at me. "Are *these* the agents that Edwin mentioned? I was expecting—"

"Yes," Lord Cabell said, interrupting his sister. "His

best agents, Louvel and Harper." Lord Cabell's eyes flashed a warning at Lady Charlotte then turned back to Harper and me. "Sir Edwin is a friend of the family. It was very good of him to send you. I understand he'll be along very soon as well?"

"Yes, though we hope to have the matter settled before then," I replied.

"And certainly before the ball," Lady Charlotte said, her eyes raking my body as she took in my armor and my mooneye once more.

Maybe I should ask her if she'd like to pet Fenton.

"Of course," I replied stiffly, staring down Lady Charlotte.

Startled by the heaviness of my own gaze, she looked away. Apparently, one could be very rich without learning how not to be very rude.

"Well, Agents, let me help. What will you need? How can we be of service?" Lord Cabell asked. "My entire household is at your disposal."

"We'll need a room where we can work," Harper said. "Somewhere quiet where we won't be disturbed. And we need to interview any witnesses of the odd events."

"Of course. Of course. Frances will see to a room for you. As for witnesses, look no further," Lord Cabell said, motioning to himself. "Please, let's sit," he added, gesturing for Harper and me to take a seat.

"You'll be in need of refreshment. Niles, please pour the agents a drink," Lady Charlotte said, motioning to a footman standing at the back of the room.

The man had been so still, I hadn't even noticed he was there.

"So, Agent Harper, what would you like to know?" Lord Cabell asked, taking a seat beside her on the divan. He turned his full attention to her.

Apparently, someone likes redheads.

Harper coughed uncomfortably and scooted away a little. She pulled her binder from her satchel and spent an extra-long moment fussing with it. "Well, to start, what can you tell us about the curse?" she asked.

Lady Charlotte sighed as though she was bored with the topic. Lord Cabell, however, took a deep—almost shuddering—breath.

Niles, the nearly invisible footman, appeared with a tray of drinks. Lord Cabell took a glass, sipped, then said, "The curse is just family lore, really. But the tale goes that our ancestor, Lord Bran Cabell, decided that the small village on the edge of our estate was actually a coven of witches. The little village had been there for centuries, and it did have some religious connection or some such, but I don't know what for certain. Nothing Christian, but no more than that. Anyway, the previous members of the Cabell family simply taxed them and went on their way. But Lord Bran Cabell destroyed the place and burned the residents on a pyre. Their leader, who legend says was the head witch, cursed him. She warned that if any heir ever stepped foot in their village again, they would die within a fortnight."

"Witches," Lady Charlotte said with a shake of the head. "I always presumed the story was intended to keep us from wandering about in the bog and drowning."

"And how long ago was it that you went to the site?" I asked.

"Six days ago." Lord Cabell sipped once more. "We are planning to put in a new steam station to draw the water away from the road. You may have noticed such stations as you flew in. They're excellent for controlling the water and preparing the land for farming. Anyway, as I was out riding, looking for sites for the new station, I traveled to the area where the village once stood. The ruins are on elevated ground. In the past, I've always ridden by, but this time I decided to have a look. The place is really ideal for a new station. Anyway, the ruins are overgrown, but there are the remains of nine small stone cabins. I don't know if the story about the witches is true or not, but someone did once live there. And…I found something odd."

"Odd how?" I asked.

"Well, the story goes that the witches were tied together and burned at the stake at the center of their village. When I was there, I found a center pyre. The coals were still hot," he said then took a drink once more. "Ever since, we have heard howling in the middle of the night. The sound is…inhuman."

Lady Charlotte scoffed. "Inhuman indeed. Agents, you must understand, I want my guests to be titillated, not terrified. To that end, I've hired tarot readers, palm readers, and a medium to hold a séance. If anything is going to evoke a little fear, I've paid for it. I don't want any distractions. No doubt Edison kicked up some wild animal or something. You handle things like that, don't you? Inconveniences?" she asked, her eyes drifting down to Fenton's pelt.

"Yes, we do," I said.

"Very good. I'm sure it's nothing, but my brother insisted we ask Edwin's help. I wasn't inclined to disagree," she said, a wistful smile passing her lips. "But if you do find anything odd, I'm sure you'll make it go away, won't you?"

I stared at her. My mind raced, unsure if I wanted to unpack that wistful smile or think about the idea that Lady Charlotte was inclined to have others make her problems just go away.

Deciding to focus on neither, I took a drink from the tray Niles was offering me. It seemed the footman knew precisely when I would need a drink.

I cast him a passing look, noting the playful sparkle in his eyes.

I lifted the drink and took a sip. As I did so, I eyed Lady Charlotte closely. Funny how even just hearing her name back in London, I knew I wasn't going to like her. My instincts rarely failed me. Lady Charlotte was pretty, rich, and spoiled. But what was, exactly, her connection with Edwin? Did they have a history? Surely, Edwin was never attached to a woman like her. Lord Cabell seemed nice enough, even if he was inching closer to Harper by the second.

"We'll need to have a look at the ruins," Harper said as she studied her notes intently. "Can someone take us out in the morning?"

Lord Cabell nodded. "The groundskeeper, Mister Aaron, will assist you there. I'll ask him to be at your disposal first thing. I'll ask Frances to arrange for you to work from the library."

"But Lord Munsford always takes in the library while he's here," Lady Charlotte complained.

"Yes, but he won't arrive for three days."

"And if the case takes longer than that? Surely the small library would be sufficient, Edison."

"Very well. The small library then. But I'm sure these agents will have this distraction in hand by the ball. "

Lady Charlotte sighed. "The whole mess is rather

vulgar. The family curse makes for a wonderfully spooky milieu until—"

"Until the wolves come howling," I said, forcing myself not to smirk.

Lady Charlotte stared at me, her eyes narrowing. "Precisely. But I suppose that's what your pistol is for," she said tartly.

"Indeed, it is."

Harper, who'd been nursing her own drink, raised her eyebrows quickly then polished off her glass, hiding her grin in the process.

Lord Cabell rose, which, of course, meant we had to stand too. I took a sip of my drink and set it aside.

"Niles will show you to the small library. Niles, be a good chap and let Frances know they'll be working from there."

"Yes, sir."

"Lady Charlotte will ask our housekeeper to see you to your rooms," Lord Cabell said.

"Oh, dear. Yes. Well, with so many guests coming and all the preparations underway, I hope you don't mind if we roomed you together," Lady Charlotte said.

"Is that really necessary?" Lord Cabell asked her.

"Yes," she replied, her gaze steely.

"Very well. The house is your ship this time of year. I'm not in residence at Cabell Manor often, Agents. My work frequently takes me abroad. In fact, I'm bound for

India soon. When I'm gone, my sister has the run of the house."

"It's no matter," I said, nodding to Lord Cabell. "We're here to work."

"You see," Lady Charlotte said. "No matter to them. Now, I'm afraid you've missed dinner, but we'll see to it that the cooks prepare you something to eat. Will sandwiches be all right?"

Death by a thousand small slights? I think not. Lady Charlotte was growing more comical by the moment.

"Anything is fine," Harper replied.

"Niles, make sure Missus Carroll sees to it," Lady Charlotte told the footman.

"Of course, m'lady," he said, bowing to her. He then turned to us. "Agents, if you will come this way."

We exited the parlor, the footman closing the door behind us. I could hear Lord Cabell and Lady Charlotte talking. The words *women* and *eye* were distinct over the other muffled proclamations.

"Well, that was…enlightening," Harper whispered as we followed the footman down the hall.

"In many ways."

"I wondered if you noticed that little smile at the mention of Agent Hunter."

"Yes, I did."

"No worries, Louvel. You have that situation all sewn up."

"You suppose so?"

"I was surprised to find upon my return that you weren't affianced already."

I blew air through my lips. "Too busy for that." *And the little issue with Lionheart.* But that didn't matter. He was gone. Hard to tell if he'd come back at all. Hard to say anything about that with him gone. When was he coming back?

"Well, I'm here now, partner. Where do we start, besides the *small* library?" Harper asked with a chuckle.

"I'd say, with another drink. Can you be of help, Niles?"

The footman looked at us over his shoulder and smirked. "Of course, Agents. And if you'll be staying awhile, I'd best bring a whole bottle."

CHAPTER 7
The Witching Hour

Harper and I spent the remainder of the evening poring over the papers we'd brought with us from the agency, the family maps of the estate, and what few ledger notes could be found regarding the coven and the curse. And enjoying our sandwiches. There wasn't much about the curse in the family records. Prior to Lord Bran's extraordinary act of violence, there were a few notes regarding the bi-annual taxes collected from the village—mainly in the form of livestock and goods. But no names, no details. Whatever had happened here long ago had mostly become part of the local folklore.

That night, a maid led Harper and me to a quiet room in a quiet corner of the house. It was a modestly appointed bedchamber, fit for the working class. Not quite a maid's chamber, but certainly not the sort of room in which one would house a fancy Lord or Lady.

"Comfy," Agent Harper said with a yawn as she settled into bed. She fluffed her pillow once or twice then lay down.

I went to the window and had a look out. The moon was nearly full, a complication, which would prove problematic if there was a pack of werewolves out there. What moonlight there was turned the landscape into dark shadows occluded by a bluish mist.

I closed my good eye and scanned the horizon. I couldn't see a damned thing. But I felt…something.

"Well?" Harper asked.

"Well, what?"

"What do you think?"

"There's something out there."

"Figured as much. The place has my hackles risen too."

"And the moon is almost full."

"I noticed that too."

"If there's a pack out here, they'll be lawless, not beholden to the realm's alpha."

"Wild and wooly. That will be fun. Speaking of alphas, have you heard anything about when Lionheart will be back?"

A tight knot formed in my stomach. "No."

"He went all the way to the Holy Land?"

"That's what they told me."

"I'm surprised."

"Surprised why?"

"I'm surprised he took it so hard. Bryony Paxton was pretty and bright and such a nice person, and I was so sorry to learn what had happened, but she and Lionheart just didn't fit."

"Ah. Well. Who knows?" *And who does he fit with?*

I turned from the window and sat down on the bed.

"What do you think we'll find out there tomorrow?" Harper asked.

"Not sure, but I do know one thing."

"Oh?"

"It won't be mummies."

"Thanks, Louvel. Now I'm going to have nightmares," Harper said with a laugh.

"Sorry." I lay down and closed my eyes. Lionheart appeared in my mind's eye once more. I saw him clearly in my memory, looking up at me from under that lock of hair, his face a mess of tangled emotions in the moment before he'd kissed me. I sighed. Maybe I'd given Harper a theme for her dreams, but her words had also infected mine.

Lionheart, come back.

I WOKE FROM A DEAD SLEEP IN THE MIDDLE OF THE NIGHT. I had been dreaming that I was standing on Glastonbury Tor—which I had only seen drawings of before. The land all around the Tor was covered in dense fog. From somewhere in the mist, a voice called my name.

I'd shuddered, feeling scared—not of the voice per se, but of what I'd find out there.

"Don't be afraid. I'm here," someone whispered, slipping their hand into mine.

I sighed with relief, my nerves calming. When I looked back, I found Lionheart there, his ruby red eyes shimmering.

The dream shook me, making me sit bolt upright in bed.

"Richard," I whispered into the night air.

Then, I heard it.

A long, low howl sounded outside. I could barely make it out over the sound of Harper's snoring.

Shaking the dream off, I slipped out of bed and shook Harper's shoulder.

"Wake up," I whispered. "Elaine, wake up."

Harper snorted hard, waking herself. Her eyes opened slowly. "Clemeny? What's wrong?"

"Listen," I said, lifting a finger.

We both stilled, and a moment later, I heard the howl once more.

"Not good," Harper said, getting out of bed. I turned

and grabbed a dressing robe, goggles, knife, and my pistols. Slipping on my boots, I headed down the hallway toward the main stairwell, Harper right behind me.

There was a grandfather clock in the hall. I noted the time as we passed: three o'clock.

"Witching hour," I told Harper.

We hurried down the steps, pausing when we got to the main foyer, so we could listen once more.

Again, the howl sounded.

"Back of the house," Harper said.

I scanned around, trying to figure out which hallway led to the back garden.

"Agents," Lord Cabell called as he rushed down the stairs. Looking bedraggled, his hair a tousled mess, he'd thrown on a velvet dressing robe. I saw him glance at our weapons, but he didn't say anything. "This way," he added, motioning us to follow him.

We all rushed down a back hallway, Lord Cabell stopping to push open a set of double doors. On the other side was the ballroom.

The place was festively decorated. There were cornstalks tied in bunches, gourds and jack-o-lanterns, autumn flowers, scarecrows, and paper-mâché ravens. Witches' caps had been suspended from the ceiling. I had to applaud Lady Charlotte's ingenuity. The place looked downright haunting.

Lord Cabell led us to a set of wide doors at the side of the ballroom that led out to a terrace at the back of the house that overlooked the garden.

The three of us stood staring into the mist. Statues of angels, their marble heads dimly lit by the moonlight, stood like silent soldiers watching stony-eyed across the garden.

Everything was so still.

I scanned the horizon, looking for anything, any sign of movement.

"Clemeny?" Harper whispered.

I closed my good eye once more, hunting for any shape in the darkness.

A howl sounded again. It was closer to the house.

"Damn mist," I whispered, pulling on my night array goggles. "Stay with Lord Cabell," I told Harper then moved down the steps into the terraced garden.

I hadn't gone ten feet when the fog swallowed me. The night optics pierced the darkness better than the naked eye, enhancing the vision of my mooneye.

My pistol in front of me, a knife in my hand, I moved slowly down the steps. Passing a winged angel, I came to a reflecting pool. I scanned all around, looking for any sign of...anything.

The palms of my hands and bottoms of my feet felt prickly.

"Come on, I know you're out here," I said, looking all around.

Not far from me, a howl sounded once more. It was a strange sound. Something about it seemed odd, different. I couldn't put my finger on how or why, but I did know it was something preternatural.

Stepping carefully, I moved toward the sound.

The mist around me rolled, moving like it was alive, confusing my optics. As I headed deeper into the mist, the fog briefly congealed into apparitions. Shapes took form. Ghosts danced through the mists. One after the other, the spirits floated by, coming in for a closer look, then dissipating almost as quickly as they appeared.

When I reached the edge of the garden, coming up on a tree line at the garden's edge, I stopped.

Somewhere beyond the trees, I heard a low, menacing growl. The sound was followed by the crunching of underbrush. Whatever it was retreated away from the house. I stood there and watched, listening to the creature escape back into the fen.

"Clemeny?" Harper called from the house.

She sounded so far away.

I stared out into the mist. There was something here, but what? The howl had been wolf-like, but I hadn't seen the tell-tale red eyes.

The fog rolled. A figure formed in the mist amongst the trees. It took on the shadowy shape of a woman. Her features were indistinct, but she wore long, flowing robes and her hair moved around her as if she was standing in the breeze.

I pulled off the night optic.

I could still make out the shadowed form, a silhouette of white. But with my mooneye, I saw the opalescent glow of the otherworld surrounding the spirit.

Clemeny, a soft female voice called. *Clemeny.*

The figure reached out toward me, her hand extended.

My skin rose in gooseflesh.

"Clemeny?" Harper called once more.

A gentle wind blew, disturbing the fog. The mist around the spirit stirred and then she dissipated, blowing back into the night air.

Right. Okay. I stared at the spot where the spirit had hovered and then I looked beyond into the fen. So, Lord Cabell most definitely had a problem. Something preternatural was keen on getting close to the house. Add to that, Cabell Manor was definitely haunted. But whatever spirits lurked, they didn't appear to be after Lord Cabell.

But they might be after me.

CHAPTER 8
The Fen

The next morning, Harper and I dressed and headed to the small library. The servants brought us a quick bite to eat as we waited for Mister Aaron, the groundskeeper, who arrived shortly thereafter.

"And you didn't see red eyes?" Harper asked for the hundredth time.

"No."

"That howl. It wasn't exactly wolf-like."

"It was odd."

"Hellhound?" Harper asked.

"Maybe."

"Don't devils have glowing eyes too?"

"Yes," I said, remembering Phillip Phillips. "What else howls?"

"Banshees wail. Could be some other weird bogey,

something we don't see much of in the city," Harper said then shook her head. "I'm not sure."

Neither was I. I hadn't told Harper about the ethereal spirit that had called my name. Whatever it had been, it didn't appear to be connected to the case. Something had been calling me for months. I had yet to discover why.

I needed to go to the summer country.

Maybe when Lionheart got back.

The door opened, and a tall gentleman entered. "Good morning, Agents. I'm Mister Aaron. I hear we're for the moor this morning." Mister Aaron was a tall man with an impressive handlebar mustache. He smiled good-naturedly at us, giving us a small bow. I couldn't help but notice that he had a shotgun resting on his shoulder.

"Yes, sir," Harper replied.

"Very well. And I presume you are armed?"

I looked at Harper. "We are. And we should be?"

"Well, I'm not sure what you're looking for out there, Agents. But Lady Charlotte asked me to bring back some duck for dinner. In your line of work, I figured the two of you would be good shots," he said with a laugh.

Harper chuckled. "That we are."

"Very well," he said then motioned for us to follow.

"Lady Charlotte is quickly getting on my last nerve," I whispered to Harper.

She chuckled. "Don't worry. They're always haughty and skeptical until some monster is breathing down their throats. Then it's all screaming, *'Help me, Harper. Help! The mummy is going to eat my eyes,'*" she said then shuddered.

"Good god, Elaine. Where in the hell did they send you?"

"Never, ever agree to go to Egypt."

Mister Aaron led us out the back of the manor into the garden. Mist swirled around the statues. Stoney-eyed stone angels peered across the landscape, looking into the unknown beyond. I scanned the garden, realizing it was mainly planted with shrubbery and trees. Not enough sunlight for blossoms. If it weren't for the howling, this seemed like a good spot for Agent Rose's friends. But the garden was remarkably calm that morning. There was no sign of spirit nor yowling beasts.

"Does the sun ever shine here?" Harper asked, frowning at the fog.

"Oh, yes. At least ten percent of the time we see sunlight," Mister Aaron said with a good-natured smile.

"We saw something outside last night. I spotted movement there," I said, pointing to the tree line. "Let's have a look. Are you a good tracker, Mister Aaron?"

"That I am."

"Well, let's go see what's been sniffing around," I said.

We went to the tree line and inspected the ground for any sign. It wasn't long before Mister Aaron found something.

"Here," he called, waving to Harper and me.

We joined him.

"Right there, as bold as brass," Mister Arron said, pointing to a paw print in the dirt. "Looks like a wolf, Agents."

Frowning, I knelt and had a closer look, as did Harper.

"Definitely an animal," I said, but the print wasn't large enough for a werewolf. Whatever it was, it had very long claws.

"A cat, maybe?" Harper asked.

"There aren't any big cats in the fens, unless you count the phantom lucifee that's been spotted from time to time."

"What's a lucifee?" Harper asked.

"A big, black cat. Like a puma or panther. Every now and then a legend pops up about it. Someone claims they spotted it. Just a local myth."

"Kind of like the Cabell family curse?" I said.

Mister Aaron chuckled lightly. "Exactly. Wolves, however, are a problem out here."

I studied the print closer. It was definitely a paw

print, but of what? But then, I noticed something odd. "Six toes," I said, motioning to the print once more. "Did you see that? Six toes."

Harper and Mister Aaron both had a closer look. Harper frowned then looked up at me, both of us thinking the same thing. Six-toed animals were rare, but there was one species of preternatural that always had six toes: a witch's familiar.

Mister Aaron took a few steps out into the fen. "It's all mire from there out," he said, pointing. "The brush is crushed down, but you can see the direction it was headed. We can't follow it that way, but whatever it was, it's headed the same direction we are. But let's take the dry path. This way, Agents," he said, hoisting his weapon onto his shoulder once more.

Mister Aaron led us across the gardens, passing through a gate on the far side. The wrought iron squeaked as we exited.

Walking down a rise, we found a narrow footpath that led into the misty fen.

"Where does this trail go?" Harper asked.

"Well, when it's not raining, you can follow it all the way to the ruins of Castle Acre. Though it might take a full day to get there. But we'll be making a turn long before," he said.

As Harper and I followed along, I scanned the landscape around me. Frogs croaked and loons called from the marsh. I wasn't sure if the trees nearby had lost their leaves because it was autumn or if they were waterlogged and dead, but what trees dotted the bog appeared lifeless. I heard the sound of a windmill and could just make out its shape in the distance. Turning back to the manor, I spotted Archangel Michael on the roof, but already everything was lost to the mist. If I hadn't known it was morning, it would be hard to tell.

We walked for quite a while when Mister Aaron stopped. "This way, and follow my steps," Mister Aaron said, turning from the path into the bog. "Be sure to step on the center of the peat. A squish one way or the other will have you in the water."

We followed Mister Aaron into the moor.

"Mister Aaron, what do you make of the family legend? Is there any truth to it?" Harper asked.

"Well," he said, drawing out the word as if in thought. "I've heard the stories about the witches and the burning. And it wouldn't surprise me a bit that such a thing happened back in those days. As for the curse..." He shrugged. "I suppose it depends on if you believe in witchcraft or not. I do not. But Lord Cabell found something. I suspect he kicked up someone squatting in the old village. In which case, all three of us being armed is a very good thing."

"Indeed," Harper agreed.

"And what about wolves," I asked. "You said they are known to be in the area."

"Oh, about six or seven years ago our neighbors over at Granfield Place—Lord Samson's lands—were troubled by a wolf pack hunting their lands. Wouldn't have minded them except they kept getting into the sheep. Samson's game warden chased the devils off. Haven't had any problems with wolves since then."

I frowned. I needed to remind myself that in the country, wolves could be just that, wolves. I was so used to walking, talking, smirking, devilishly handsome beasts that I could hardly conceive of a regular canine.

"Were you with Lord Cabell when he discovered evidence that someone had been at the ruins?" Harper asked.

"No, I was not. Lord Cabell knows the land as well as I do. He was out on his own. Though I dare say, if I were him, I wouldn't have tempted fate."

"Didn't you just say you don't believe in witchcraft?" I asked.

"I don't. But ruffians I know well," he said, patting his gun.

Ruffians made sense, but that still didn't explain the howls or the paw print. There may very well be ruffians on the property, but not the kind he thought.

It took two hours before we finally came to a rise in the landscape, the ground sloping upward around a bank in the earth. I didn't need to see the rise to know we were there. The palms of my hands and the bottoms of my feet hand been tingling for the last ten minutes. The boggy path suddenly gave way to a clear, albeit overgrown, road that led toward the rise.

"Look," Harper said, motioning to the path that led up to the ruins. Alongside the path, about the same height as a man, were standing stones. Harper went ahead to investigate. Brushing some lichen away, she inspected the stone. "Ogham…and Celtic symbols," she said. "Very old." She looked up the hill, counting. "There are nine stones."

I tried to ignore the fact that my skin had risen to gooseflesh and the hair on my head felt like it had been struck by lightning.

"How long has the settlement been here?" I asked Mister Aaron.

"You are in the land of the Iceni, ladies. There have been tribes here for centuries. Some say that when the Romans finally crushed the Iceni after Boudica's raid, many of her tribe members retreated into the fens where the Romans couldn't find them. But who knows. There has always been lore about the old Celts in these parts."

"And what about lore of druids?" Harper asked. She

went to the next monolith, inspecting the markings thereon.

"Old tales, that's all," he said then shrugged. "Where didn't the old Celtic tribes and the druids roam once?"

Frowning, Harper pulled out her journal and quickly jotted down some notes.

"The ruins are just at the top of the rise," Mister Aaron said. "May I suggest caution?" he added, motioning to his shotgun.

I nodded, pulling my pistols.

Harper took one last note then slipped her notepad back in her bag. She pulled her pistol from her shoulder holster.

I inhaled deeply, blowing out my breath slow and steady. I joined Mister Aaron. It didn't matter how good a huntsman he was if he wasn't carrying silver bullets.

We rounded the rise, passing more standing stones, then found ourselves standing at the entrance of a settlement. Two massive old oak trees stood sentinel at the entrance to the place. Their leaves held the last tints of autumn orange. The ground below my feet was covered in leaves and acorns. Glancing around the site, I noted there were nine small, stone structures there. Five of them were nothing more than walls. The other four, however, were overgrown with vines. One even looked like it might still have some timbers inside and seemed suitable for hiding.

The three of us stood perfectly still as we listened for any sign.

I cast a glace about, letting my mooneye do its work. There was something here. I could feel it, but I couldn't see anything.

"Look," Harper whispered, motioning toward the center of the settlement. I spotted a bank of coals near the pyre. There was a light scent of smoke in the air, the coals glimmering orange and white.

"Well, Lord Cabell is right. There is someone here," Mister Aaron whispered.

"Or was, very recently," Harper said.

"We need to check the structures," I said, motioning to the buildings. "Harper, stay with Mister Aaron and take the buildings on the right."

She nodded, and they set off to examine the ruins.

Slipping one of my pistols back into its holster, I pulled my blade and headed toward the first structure. Part of the wall had fallen down. Listening for any sound of movement, I slipped inside to find nothing more than leaves, spiders, and a forgotten hearth. Some pieces of furniture lay in ruins beside the old stone fireplace. Nothing here had been disturbed.

I crawled back out, casting a glance toward Harper and Mister Aaron. Having completed their inspection, Harper reemerged from inside the dilapidated structure.

I met her glance.

Harper shook her head.

I moved across the space toward the other building, which looked far more promising. As I went, my palms began to tingle. I checked my weapon once more and drew close.

Clemeny...

Clemeny...

From somewhere beyond the building, somewhere below the rise and out in the fen, a soft, feminine voice called out to me.

My stomach clenched.

No. Not now. Not that.

I forced myself to stay calm and moved toward the building. The ground in front of the entrance had been disturbed, the vines and leaves were broken and unsettled. Walking carefully, I stepped inside.

There was a rustle in the back of the structure, and a moment later, something came hurtling toward me.

"What the hell?" I said, blocking whatever was headed my way with my hands.

Something small slammed into me, then pushed around me and back outside, making a terrible racket as it went.

I turned to find a pheasant escaping.

Harper looked from me to the bird. Mister Aaron lifted his shotgun. He took aim at the bird. But in the split second before he fired, something back inside the building rustled.

"Hell's bells."

Mister Aaron shot, the sound of the blast echoing across the moor.

I turned and went back into the house. The ivy covering a hole in the wall at the very back of the structure was swishing back and forth. Moving quickly, I dashed across the room and looked out the gap in the back of the building. The mist beyond the hovel moved as if it had been disturbed by someone rushing through.

Following quickly, I rushed through the mist, chasing something I could not see. The only evidence of their wake was the rolling fog and the tingling in my palms.

Clemeny…

Clemeny…

I raced down the rise to the bog below. Watching my step, I followed the movement of the mist. Someone or something was just ahead of me. I rushed into the swamp. For just a brief moment, I saw the silhouette of someone, but they turned and ran off.

"Clem? Clemeny, where are you?" Harper called from ruins above.

I rushed forward, mindful of my steps, out into the fen. But soon, the fog settled. Everything around me became very still. There was no sign of the other person. I scanned around, looking, listening.

But there was nothing.

"Clemeny?" Harper called, her voice echoing through the mist.

A soft wind blew, carrying with it the heavy scents of mud and peat.

The breeze blew away the mist to reveal that I was standing in the middle of a ring of stones.

CHAPTER 9
The Land of the Iceni

"Clem? Clemeny?" Harper called, and this time I heard the worry in her voice.

"I'm here. I'm coming back now," I yelled back.

My skin rose in gooseflesh. I scanned around, looking at the stones. There were nine pairs in all, capped like doorways, each carved with elaborate symbols. There was a sheen on the stones, dampness from the mist, which gave them an odd, bluish sparkle.

My heart beating hard, I stepped toward the center of the ring where a stone altar had been erected.

I could see a rudely carved basket sitting thereon.

I approached slowly, feeling someone's—or something's—eyes on me. Pausing, I peered into the mist once more. I couldn't see anything.

"I know you're there," I said.

I closed my good eye and panned all around. My mooneye was playing tricks on me, seeing fleeting shadows in the air around me. Balls of light, silhouettes, undefined shapes moved through the mist. But what did I expect? I was standing at the gateway of the shadowlands.

Stepping close to the altar, I braced myself then looked into the basket.

Within were a dead hare, some apples, and wild mushrooms.

A sacrifice?

An offering?

Given the condition of the hare, it was clear that someone had been here not long ago. Was it the same person in the ruined building or someone different?

I frowned.

Clemeny, a feminine voice called, no lighter than the wind, rustling my hair as if someone had breathed my name onto the back of my neck.

My skin rose to gooseflesh. "What do you want from me?"

Soft laughter floated on the breeze.

I turned around.

There was no one there.

I holstered my weapons. Glancing at the basket once

more, I decided to leave it. The old, Celtic gods had once ruled the land. While I'd spent my childhood in Saint Clement Danes and had felt the presence of the divine on more than one occasion, I'd always had some doubts. How and why did the gods disappear? Can a god really disappear? If people stop believing, does that mean the gods never existed, or does that mean they are simply forgotten? There were a lot of things roaming about our realm that people didn't believe in. But they were real. Real enough to plant a kiss on my lips. And if werewolves and vampires and goblins were real, what else was real? I looked at the basket once more. Real or not, I knew better than to touch an offering left to the gods.

WATCHING MY STEP, I WALKED BACK TOWARD THE RISE. To my surprise, I noticed a sloping path that lead back to the village. I followed the trail, noting the menhirs that dotted this side of the settlement just as they did the other. And once more, there were nine stones. I returned to the ruins to find Mister Aaron collecting the pheasant and Harper staring at the hovel where I'd disappeared. She was frowning heavily.

"Well?" I asked. "Scowl any answers out of it?"

Harper breathed an audible sigh of relief. "Where did you go?"

"Chasing someone...or something."

"Which was it—a someone or a something?"

"Lines are blurry on that topic, aren't they?"

Harper rolled her eyes at me.

"A someone, I think. But I didn't get a good look. I did, however, find a miniature Stonehenge on the other side of that rise," I said, pointing toward the mist.

"There are a good number of standing stones hereabouts," Mister Aaron said. "Most of them are overgrown or have fallen down, some half sunk into the fen. There are three more rings of stones on the Cabell estate, in fact."

"Does anyone attend to them?" Harper asked.

"Lord Cabell's father tried—put a fence around one of them, but it fell apart, and no one ever bothered to repair it. Every once in a while, someone will come down from Oxford or Cambridge to have a look. Otherwise, no one much bothers with them."

"I think your theory about the Iceni might hold some weight, Mister Aaron," Harper said.

He nodded. "Lots of evidence of early life on the fens, if you know where to look, and if the bog doesn't swallow you whole first."

"Seems a good place to hide from the Romans," Harper said.

"Or from religious persecution," I added under my breath.

Harper flicked her eyes toward me but said nothing.

"Indeed," Mister Aaron said. "So, what did you kick up, Agent Louvel?" Mister Aaron asked.

"Can't say, exactly. Fox, maybe. Whatever it was, I lost it in the mist."

Mister Aaron stroked his ample mustache. "Tracks are a bit small for a fox. But the beast could have pinned the bird in there. All the better for us, I suppose," he said, holding up the pheasant, gazing at it with pride.

I smiled.

"Shall we head back now?" Harper asked. Her question surprised me. I had expected Harper to want to examine every square inch of the place. As for me, I could feel that there were answers here. I looked over my shoulder toward the ring. The answers, however, were just beyond my grasp. But something told me if I wanted to know what was haunting Cabell Manor, I would need to come out at night.

"Very good," Mister Aaron said, then motioned for us to follow along behind him as he led us back toward the entrance of the ruins. "We should still have enough time to get some duck hunting in along the way."

Harper chuckled, and we turned to follow Mister Aaron.

Harper fell back to join me. "I think it might be wise

to come back here at night. Preferably alone," she whispered.

I smiled, feeling proud of my partner's good instincts. "I was thinking the same thing."

"Really, Clemeny. A fox?" Harper scoffed.

"Well, he almost believed me," I said then tapped my temple. "Wiley like a fox, at least."

"What was it? A person?"

"I think so."

"What about the stones?"

"Someone has been there recently."

"How do you know?"

"Well, first, I could feel their eyes on me. And then there was the offering they left on the altar."

Harper stopped. "An offering?"

I nodded, took her by the arm, and moved forward.

"Was it bad?" she asked, scrunching up her nose as if she was preparing herself for a tale of the macabre.

I chuckled. "Egypt certainly did a number on your imagination. No mutilated corpses, just a basket with a hare, apples, and mushrooms. An offering for the gods, not entrails."

Harper sighed with relief. "I suddenly envisioned us chasing occultists through the mist, a prospect that didn't sound appealing. Apples, however, I can handle. Who left it then? And why?"

I shook my head. "I don't know, but Mister Aaron is right about one thing."

"That is?"

"If a person wanted to hide, there would be no better place do it," I said then looked behind me toward the ruins, which were now engulfed in the mist.

CHAPTER 10
Missing Pieces

When we returned to Cabell Manor, we headed to the small library and got to work. Harper began poring over her notes while I went through the Cabell family ledgers once more.

"Well, as we suspected, witch seems to be a bit of a misnomer," Harper said as she paged through her notes.

I raised an eyebrow at her.

"The stones," she said, tapping her pen on her paper. "Maybe by the sixteenth century people were calling them witches, but that was a druid's grove."

"Yes," I said as I turned the yellowed pages of the family notes. "But that doesn't explain what our six-toed friend is doing roaming about the moor, leaving sacrifices for the gods, and keeping the fire warm."

"Assuming it's the same being up to all those things. I'm no expert on druids, but can they shapeshift?" Harper asked.

I paused. "I don't know. Maybe? Their connection to animals—like a familiar—is strong."

Harper frowned. "We're missing something. Either that, or there is a shape-shifting immortal druid on the moor."

I frowned. Harper was right. The pieces weren't coming together just yet. Whatever the answer was, it was still out in the bog.

The door handle rattled, and Niles the footman opened the door. Lady Charlotte sauntered into the room, a picture of Victorian high fashion in her satin and bows.

Harper and I both rose.

"Agents, I was wondering if you would join my brother and me for dinner this evening? We're both very interested to see what you've discovered."

"Thank you, Lady Charlotte," Harper said. "We'd be delighted."

Maybe Harper would be delighted, but I had work to do, and Lady Charlotte irritated me.

"Very well. You'll hear the dressing gong around seven," Lady Charlotte said then turned, her dress making an audible swish, as she left the room. Niles passed us a knowing glance then closed the door behind her.

I frowned at Harper.

"What? We need to eat. And if my suspicions are right, you need to get used to moving in better society, Louvel," she said with a wink.

"And *that* is better society? I'd rather have dinner in the Dark District," I retorted then turned back to my papers, but now my mind was distracted. Edwin Hunter was a demon hunter and an agent. That was the Edwin I knew and cared about. Sir Edwin Hunter, the baronet, was someone else entirely. But Harper was right. As Edwin's…whatever I was…I would need to learn the ropes of polite society. After all, Edwin was close with the Queen. And while I liked Her Majesty, something told me that Victoria's knowing about our work, knowing what we faced, made her more sympathetic than someone like Lady Charlotte. I suspected Lady Charlotte would enjoy watching me struggle with the flatware. I'd hate to disappoint her, but Felice Louvel had taught her granddaughter the manners of a princess. I could even manage a waltz—if I was forced.

I turned back to my notes. Lady Charlotte was nothing. Once I had whatever monster was lurking out there on a rope, she'd be sure to change her tune.

"You need to go to bed early tonight," I told Harper.

"Why?"

"Because we'll need to be ready to chase down whatever is prowling at the witching hour."

"Wonderful. You know, we're very likely to drown out there."

"Not at all. This time, we know where to look."

"The ruins at night. This is going to be fun."

"What's the worst that can happen? It's not like we're going to find any mummies out there."

"Ha. Ha," Harper said then shuddered once more.

Harper and I stayed in the library a bit longer, studying over our notes. Harper asked the butler, Frances, to help her find a few more ledgers while I headed back to the garden. The answers we were seeking weren't in the pages of a book. They were alive and well and on the fen.

I retraced my steps, returning to the tree line where we'd found the paw print that morning. I bent low, studying the mark. I looked from the paw print toward the misty fen. Someone was out there. But who and why?

Moving carefully, I walked out into the fen. But the trail quickly grew cold, swallowed by the muddy marsh. Tonight, I would find whatever was lurking. And if it had red eyes, I was going to give it a good talking to.

The sun was low, casting hues of marigold and plum on the horizon. Pulling out my pocket watch, I noted the time, six-fifteen. Ugh. The sooner I was done with this case the better.

I turned and headed back to the house in time to dress for dinner.

CHAPTER 11
I'd Prefer A Mad Tea Party

I never much liked the blue dress Phillip Phillips had the courtesy of ruining for me. The green dress I wore during the holiday season, however, still fit just as it did years past when Grand-mère dragged me from one social event or the other. It wasn't exactly the right gown for the season, and I was sure Lady Charlotte would notice, but dinner fashion wasn't on the forefront of my mind. The six-toed critter roaming the moors, however, was.

I returned to my room to find Harper struggling to dress while a proper lady's maid, who kept calling Harper "m'lady," wrestled her for the task.

"Let me finish the buttons, m'lady," the girl told Harper as she helped my reluctant partner into a fashionable dark purple gown.

"Clemeny. There you are. I was starting to worry. They rang the dressing gong not long ago. We should get ready," Harper said, a tinge of nervous exasperation in her voice.

"I set out both your gowns, m'lady," the maid said, turning and dropping me a curtsey. "The red gown is for the ball?"

"Yes," I replied, eyeing the garment peeking at me from the wardrobe. The sight of it made a knot form in my stomach. My green gown lay on the bed.

"This is Emma," Harper said, introducing the maid who dropped a curtsey. "I told her we didn't need any help, but she insisted."

"Agent Harper is just being kind, but Lady Charlotte told Missus Carroll to send me up. I'm almost done with Agent Harper. I can assist you next, Agent Louvel. I dare say, we've never had any agents of Her Majesty's Red Capes here except Sir Edwin. How exciting."

"Does Sir Edwin dine here often?" I asked.

"Not much recently, but in earlier years, yes. He and Sir Edison get along quite well."

"And Lady Charlotte, did she get along with Sir Edwin quite well too?" Harper asked, sparing me the embarrassment of being overly nosey about Edwin's past.

"The three are always very merry in one another's company. The late Lady Cabell liked Sir Edwin very much. And Sir Edwin's godmother, Lady Chadwick, often comes to visit."

Godmother?

"I see," Harper said, giving me a knowing look.

"But I don't remember seeing Sir Edwin here since the last ball," the maid mused as she finished the last lace on Harper's gown.

I suddenly felt like I was sinking into the fen. So, Sir Edwin and Lady Charlotte had a bit of history. I suspected as much. After all, he was *Sir* Edwin, and she was *Lady* Charlotte. Of course, they'd consider a match if the families liked one another, especially this mysterious godmother whom Edwin never bothered to mention.

I suddenly felt very annoyed with Edwin.

My eyes flicked to the red dress once more. Again, the image of Lionheart looking up at me from under that lock of blond hair crossed my mind, my stomach twisting with the memory of him.

Hell's bells. Was he ever going to come back? I needed him to just come back already.

"There you are, Agent Harper," the maid said as she tied the last lace on Harper's dress. "Do you need anything else?"

Harper gave the dress a spin. "Well, what do you think?" she asked me.

"Fetching," I said with a smile. In truth, she looked

very pretty. The purple gown, trimmed with black lace and lovely beadwork, made Harper's eyes sparkle

"Good. I spent a month's salary buying two dresses just to come here. I didn't want to embarrass myself," Harper said with a laugh that the maid and I both joined.

"They meet in the parlor before dinner if you'd like to do down while I dress Agent Louvel," Emma said.

Harper nodded. "Shall I go warm them up?"

"Please."

Harper nodded to me then headed out.

I turned to the maid. "Well, let's see what you can do to make this one-eyed pirate presentable."

"How did you—if you don't mind me asking—how did it happen?" she asked, casting a glance at my mooneye.

"I got into a tangle with a wolf."

The girl laughed, but when she saw my sincere expression, she paused. "Seriously?"

"Yes. Seriously."

"That's horrifying."

"It certainly was. But I got the better of him in the end."

"You're so brave, Agent Louvel."

"Maybe. But I'd rather go fight another wolf than go downstairs for dinner."

The girl giggled. "Lord Edison is very kind. Never mind Lady Charlotte. She's all bluster and show, just like her mother was before her."

I gave the girl a knowing wink then started to strip off my armor. It was going to be a very long night.

Finally looking somewhat presentable, I headed to the parlor. The maid had pulled up my hair, affixing it with the small butterfly pin Grand-mère had sent. The little pin, which was clockwork in design, worked in such a manner that the wings wagged gently up and down. It looked a little like I was going around with a bug in my hair, but Grand-mère insisted it was fashionable. So there I was, in my Christmas gown with a torn hem and a burn on the sleeve, in October, with a bug on my head, about to have dinner with the fashionable Lady Charlotte.

A footman opened the door for me, and I entered to find Lord Cabell, Lady Charlotte, Harper, and an older gentleman I didn't recognize waiting for me.

"Ah, Agent Louvel. Very good. We were worried about you," Lady Charlotte said. "It's nearly time to go in."

"My apologies. I returned from the fens a bit late."

Lady Charlotte smiled, but I saw lines of annoyance around her eyes. "No matter. May I present our nearest neighbor, Lord Samson? We invited him to dine tonight."

I inclined my head to the man. From his elegant manner and the way he was looking down his nose at me, I could tell he was a man of means and title. "Sir."

"Agent Louvel, was it?" he asked, the snobbery in his voice as thick as gravy.

"Yes, sir."

He shrugged, raising and lowering his brows in the process. "Two lady agents. Well, Edison, can't be much to worry about if they've sent two ladies along to investigate."

"Sir Edwin tells me they are the best on his team," Lord Cabell said, smiling apologetically toward Harper and me.

"Indeed? Well, if he says so, but Sir Edwin has always been something of an odd duck," he said then turned to Lady Charlotte. "How lovely you look tonight, my dear."

I gave Lady Charlotte a once-over. She was wearing a chocolate-colored gown with elegant beading and lace. The gold, silver, and bronze-toned beads on her bodice were sewn in the shape of leaves. She wore a small comb with golden oak leaves in her hair.

"Why thank you, Lord Samson," she said, smoothing down the front of her gown. "It's nothing."

Nothing. Just perfectly in line with the season and of the latest fashion. Nothing at all.

"Dinner is served," Frances, the butler called from the door, motioning for us to adjourn to the dining room.

"Ladies," Lord Cabell said, extending his arm to Harper. He led her from the parlor, the pair walking just ahead of me. A moment later, I heard Lord Cabell say, "You're looking very lovely tonight, Agent Harper."

"Oh," Harper said as though she'd been caught off guard. "Um. Thank you."

The rest of their conversation was drowned out by the sound of Lady Charlotte complaining to Lord Samson as they walked behind me.

"It's such a disruption to the ball preparations, but it can't be helped, I suppose," she said, sounding exasperated.

"Have they found anything at all?" Lord Samson asked.

"Not yet."

Lord Samson harrumphed.

"I know, I know," Lady Charlotte said then sighed. "Hopefully Mister Aaron finds whatever it is out there prowling about and just shoots the bloody thing."

"No doubt he will. I'm sure it's nothing to worry about."

"Yes, well, we shall see what the *agents* discover," she said. And while she was behind me, I could practically hear her roll her eyes.

"There, there," Sir Samson said sympathetically.

Lady Charlotte giggled lightly.

Yep, definitely disliked Lady Charlotte. Most definitely.

"Oh! Agent Louvel, hold a moment, my dear. I think you brought in something from outside with you. Is there something in your hair?" Lady Charlotte asked, gently taking my arm.

I paused, turning to her. "Sorry?"

"I think... Is that an insect?" she asked, reaching toward the pin.

I lifted my hand to my hair. "It's... Oh. No. It's a clockwork butterfly."

Lady Charlotte pulled her hand back and stared. "Oh, yes, I see now. Heavens. That's very...whimsical."

"Indeed it is, indeed it is," Lord Samson agreed.

"Charlotte?" Edison asked. "Anything the matter?"

"No, no. False alarm," Lady Charlotte said. When she let me go, I saw her eyes dance over the sleeve of my gown, noticing the burn stain thereon. For a brief moment, she wrinkled up her nose, but her better breeding made her catch herself, and she forced on a smile. "My mistake. Let's go in."

My emotions swishing from rage to humiliation, I turned from her and headed into the elegant dining room.

Yep, definitely hated Lady Charlotte.

CHAPTER 12

At Least She Knows it's Not a Dinglehopper

While I'd been exposed to many gruesome ways to die—sucked dry by a vampire, throat chewed out by a werewolf, spooked to death by a spirit, and even cursed by fairy magic—I never knew death by dinner party was a possibility.

I stayed quiet, enjoying the sumptuous meal—mutton, fish, rabbit, truffles, and more wine than I had any business drinking—listening to Lord Samson and Lady Charlotte talk for an hour about almost nothing while Harper and Lord Cabell discovered a shared interest in farming, clockwork windmills, and a taste for travel abroad. As I ate, I gazed around the fancy dining room, taking in the elaborate candelabras, the table dressed with grape vines and coordinated purple and green flowers, and watched the footman as they worked, wondering for the first time whether or not any of the fleet of servants happened to have six fingers. Like ghosts prowling along the edges of the seen world, the staff had made themselves so invisible I'd forgotten to even question them.

Rookie mistake.

"You're lost in thought, Agent Louvel," Lord Cabell said. "I'm afraid we're odd-numbered tonight. I'm sorry we've left you in want of a dinner partner."

I choked down a chuckle. *Dinner partner. How absurd.* "Not at all. I was just thinking through the case. Would you mind if I question the servants after dinner?"

"The servants?" Lady Charlotte asked.

"No cause for alarm, Lady Charlotte. I just wanted to see if they have seen or heard anything."

"Of course," Lord Cabell said then turned to the butler. "Frances, can you ask the servants to stay in the hall after their dinner?"

I looked at Frances, a dignified man with white hair and perfect posture.

He coughed lightly, swallowing any misgivings he had, and said, "Of course, sir."

"Lord Samson," Harper said, turning her attention to the gentleman. "Lord Cabell tells me your property touches the Cabell estate."

"So it does."

"And have you ever had any troubles on your property?"

"No," Lord Samson said with a shake of the head. "Thank heavens, no. But the Samsons were not involved in that matter back in the sixteenth century."

"Thus, not cursed," Lord Cabell said, his tone a bit darker than I expected.

"Are any standing stones on your property?"

Sir Samson thought for a moment. "There was a ring of stones out there at one time, but they were pulled down and incorporated into the foundation of the village church."

"How very heathen. I'm surprised it was permitted," Lady Charlotte said, sipping her wine.

"Heathen, but practical," Lord Samson said with a laugh. "Cabell Manor is a bit more rural than Granfield Place. Our estate is quiet—dreadfully quiet—which is why my wife and daughter are both in London."

"But they'll be back in time for the ball?" Lady Charlotte asked.

"Of course, of course."

"Didn't you have some trouble a few years back, though?" Lord Cabell asked. "Someone poaching on the property?"

"Oh yes. There was that. The poaching. For a stretch of time, six or seven years back, someone was poaching my sheep. But my tenant saw to that. He and some of the lads removed some vagabonds from an unused farmstead. Nothing occult about it. Simple vagrants."

Harper nodded. "About seven year ago?"

"Yes. From what I remember, the trouble went on for a bit until we found the culprits."

"And when they were found, did they go quietly?" Harper asked.

"Indeed they did. And all the better for them. I was going to have them all arrested, but they were gone before we came around with the local law."

"That's a relief. Luckily, we've never had any vagrants here, so to speak," Lady Charlotte said.

"No, just howling hellhounds."

"Edison, don't be so morbid. Ah, here is the pudding," Lady Charlotte said, clapping her hands together as a footman arrived with a truly delicious looking confection.

I was following a train of thought, my mind puzzling over Lady Charlotte's choice of words—*we've never had any vagrants here, so to speak*—when the dessert arrived. The sight of cherries and icing on the delicious looking pudding made whatever I was chasing vanish in a puff.

When the footman set my dessert plate in front of me, I felt happy for the first time since the dinner began —despite the pudding's disappointing portion size. I slid my spoon into the dessert then took a massive bite, clearing half the plate in the process. The tastes of sugar, molasses, and spice lingered on my tongue. And in that moment, I didn't even care that Lady Charlotte had tried to embarrass me. Nothing sweeter had ever met my lips.

Well, maybe, save a kiss.

CHAPTER 13
Meanwhile, Downstairs

After dinner, Lord Samson and Lord Cabell went off for cigars and brandy. Harper, bless her, went with Lady Charlotte for a digestif, and I escaped with Frances the butler down the back stairs to the servants' hall. For the first time since I'd arrived, I heard genuinely happy laughter in the house.

"Busy place," I commented to Mister Frances.

Maids and footmen rushed up and down the hallway.

"With the ball coming, we're all hard at work preparing the rooms, the ballroom, the décor, the food… It takes days to prepare for just one night."

I passed a workroom where a maid was busy arranging bouquets. The valet and a footman were in the next room ironing and mending clothes. In a third room, two young lads were busy hollowing out pumpkins and gourds and carving the faces of jack-o-lanterns. Mister Frances led me to the servants' dining room at the very back of the house.

"One moment," he said then rang a chime summoning the servants to the room.

The servants' section quieted, and a few moments later, the servants entered their dining hall, all of them eyeing me skeptically.

There were twelve servants in all. Mister Aaron was missing, but I already knew his story. Niles, the sympathetic footman, was there, as was Emma, the young maid who'd attended Harper and me. The servants whispered to one another as they cast suspicious glances at me.

"Sorry to disrupt your work. This is Agent Louvel of Her Majesty's..." Lawrence began then trailed off, at a loss for words.

"Of Her Majesty's Red Cape Society," I finished for him. "I have just a few questions, if you don't mind."

"What about?" a younger, blond-haired footman asked.

"Don't get fresh, Bryant. Agent Louvel is here investigating the odd noises in the fen," Mister Frances answered.

"The curse," one of the kitchen maids whispered, her eyes wide.

I nodded. "Yes, the curse. I was wondering if any of you have heard the strange sounds in the fen at night?"

They all looked at one another cautiously then nodded—all of them.

"Have any of you ever seen anything?" I asked.

The head cook, a sweating woman in an apron, crossed herself. "Heavens, no."

I looked at the others, meeting each of their gazes in turn. As I scanned them, I focused with my mooneye, looking for any tremor or glow. The ones who met my eyes looked scared, staring at my scarred face and me suspiciously. The others quickly met my eyes then looked nervously away.

"Heard, yes. Seen, no," Bryant, the outspoken footman, said looking around at the others who nodded in agreement.

"So no one has seen anything?" I asked.

Everyone shook their heads.

"Is this all the staff?" I asked Mister Frances.

"There is Mister Marrow, the gardener, but he's gone to bed already. Save Mister Aaron, whom you met this morning, yes."

"I have an odd request. Please forgive me. As you can guess, in my line of work, we are prone to ask unusual questions. But, if you please, would you all mind holding out your hands—no gloves—for a brief inspection?"

"What for?" Bryant asked.

"Silence, Bryant," Lawrence said, scolding the boy. "Please do as Agent Louvel requests."

Now, more nervous than ever, all the servants held out their hands in front of them.

I took a deep breath then made my way around the room. One of them could easily be a shifter. If they were good at the game, they could have learned how to hide it. A witch, in the nineteenth-century sense of the word, would be almost impossible to detect. I didn't get the feeling that any practitioners of black magic were present, and I didn't feel the tell-tale signs that one of the preternatural was in our midst, but there was something here. I felt something…odd. Someone's gaze carried the heaviness of magic. Someone in the room knew something that they weren't telling.

"Beg your pardon, m'lady, I've been cooking all day," the kitchen maid said when I glanced over her flour-covered hands.

I smiled at her. "Please, no 'm'lady' needed here. Did you happen to make the pudding tonight?"

The girl beamed a smile at me. "I did. Did you like it?"

Ten fingers.

"It was perfect," I said with a smile. "Wouldn't happen to have any left, would you?"

"We do. Emma can bring you an extra plate," the girl said with a grin.

"With a normal person's sized serving this time," I said with a laugh.

The others chuckled, and I felt some of the tension in the room lift.

"If you liked that, wait until the ball," the head cook, who was standing just beside the girl, told me.

"I can hardly wait. I admit I have a weakness for sweets," I said with a smile as I glanced over her hands.

Ten fingers.

"Well, there are worse vices in the world," Bryant, who was standing beside to cook, told me.

"Indeed?" I asked with a playful smile.

To my surprise, he winked at me.

Ten fingers.

"Cheeky," I chided him with a chuckle then moved on around the circle.

I rounded the room, inspecting the housemaids, kitchen boys, and others. One after the other, I found ten fingers. It occurred to me to ask to see their toes as well, but if there was a six-toed shifter in the group, they'd already know what I was looking for and this little exercise would out them well enough without having to embarrass the ladies by asking them to take off their stockings.

"How will you catch whatever is out there?" one of

the maids, a nervous looking girl with black hair and dark brown eyes asked.

"Hard to say. Depends on what's out there. But I believe we're coming around to some conclusions," I said, giving the girl a hard look.

Ten fingers.

I lingered before the girl. She wouldn't meet my eyes. She was no shifter, but there was something here.

"What's your name, love?" I asked the girl.

"Kerry, m'lady—er, Agent."

"Kerry, how long have you been working at Cabell Manor?"

"Kerry has been with us two years, Agent Louvell," Missus Carroll, the housekeeper, answered for her.

"Are you from around here?"

"Ye-yes. The village."

"Kerry's mother is the village apothecary," Missus Carroll explained.

I raised an eyebrow at Missus Carroll.

"She's a shy girl, Agent Louvel," Missus Carroll said.

"And a sweet girl," the head cook added.

I smiled reassuringly at them all.

"No need to worry," I said, setting my hand on the girl's shoulder. "I was just curious."

As I had gone around the room, I had slipped the silver knucklebuster in my pocket onto my hand. If the girl had been a shifter, my touch—and the silver—would have affected her. But it didn't. She wasn't a shifter, but she knew something. Maybe she was just a shy girl, but those dark eyes were heavy. They had seen magic.

"Thank you all for your patience," I told them. "Agent Harper and I will have the matter in hand in no time. But if anyone sees anything, or if you remember anything, please don't hesitate to tell Agent Harper or me. We don't bite," I said, casting a glance around the room then back to the girl.

She nodded but still didn't look up.

I turned to Mister Frances. "I'm sorry to worry you and to interrupt your work. I'm done here."

"Not to worry, Agent Louvel. Back to work, everyone," Mister Frances told the others then motioned for me to follow him. We headed back down the hall away from the servants who erupted into a flurry of whispered conversation in my wake.

"Don't mind Kerry, Agent. She is a sweet young thing, just a bit timid."

"Of course."

"Do you need anything else, Agent?"

"Yes. Any chance you can smuggle me back into the library. I have some work to do."

Mister Frances laughed. "Subterfuge is a servant's expertise, Agent Louvel."

I cast a glance over my shoulder, back down the hallway toward the servant's hall. Kerry was still there. Her eyes followed me. The cook clapped the girl on her shoulder.

Kerry gave her a soft smile then looked back at me.

I felt the weight of her dark eyes on me.

"Indeed?" I replied to Mister Frances. "That's very good to know."

He chuckled.

The girl looked away.

Well, at least some of the pieces were finally coming together.

CHAPTER 14
The Night Shift

I spent the night working in the library and doing my best to avoid Lady Charlotte. It was nearly ten when Harper finally appeared.

"I thought you went to bed," she told me. "Slunk back here and left me to Lady Charlotte, eh? Thanks for that."

"Well, we must all make sacrifices on behalf of the case."

Harper scanned the table. "Is that... Did you have more pudding?"

"The cook was kind enough to send me a human-sized portion."

"And you didn't ask for one for me?"

I pointed to the second empty plate on the table.

"That's low, Louvel," Harper said, frowning at me. She slumped into one of the oversized wingback leather chairs. "My head is blasting. Once the men joined us, everyone started drinking wine—again. The posh are such lushes."

I chuckled. "Quinn gave me a golden piece of advice. Never, whether pressured by the posh or when flirting with a brawny Scottish tapster, drink on the job."

Harper pressed her fingertips to her temples. "Now you tell me. Wait, a brawny Scottish tapster? That explains a lot," she said then winked at me.

I chuckled. "Why don't you go up to bed?"

"Are you just trying to get rid of me because you have another dessert coming?"

"I would never do that."

"I don't want to miss all the howling."

"You sure about that? If so, you better have a cup of coffee. But I suggest you go to bed. Go sleep so you can help me tromp through the fens again tomorrow. And we may need to take a trip to the village."

"What for?"

"A trip to the apothecary."

Harper rose, her hand drifting to her stomach. "A trip to the apothecary sounds like an excellent idea. Ugh."

"Good lord, Harper. How much did you drink?"

"Well, they served a glass with each course. And then afterward too."

"I don't think you're supposed to drink a full glass with each. Sip. Next time, sip. Now, go to bed."

"Sip." She nodded. "I'll remember that for next time. Oh! The servants. Did you find our six-toed friend?"

"Well, there was no shooting and nothing is on fire, so not yet. But I do believe we have a magic user in our midst."

Harper wrinkled up her nose. "Doesn't mean they're connected to the case. Who?"

"A kitchen maid."

"Could be she's just a medium or something. Did you ask?"

"No, not in front of the others. The girl looked like she wanted to jump out of her skin."

"Even out here, the Red Capes would be feared by anyone trying to stay out of sight. You know better than anyone that not all preternaturals are bad."

No, they weren't all bad. Some were quite the opposite.

"True. Either way, she's one to keep an eye on."

"Clemeny, is the room spinning?"

I chuckled. "No. And you'd better sit down before you vomit all over the Cabell's fine Turkish rugs."

Harper nodded in agreement then dropped back into the chair.

I shook my head then turned back to my notes. There was something here, something just out of my grasp. What was going on here?

"Clemeny, if I die, take my body home to my mother," Harper said a little while later, her voice a half-groan, half-whisper.

"Want to know the worst part?"

"Huh?" she replied weakly.

"You're going to live."

I SIPPED COFFEE AND LISTENED TO HARPER SNORE AS I looked over my notes and waited for time to pass. What I didn't understand was why the Cabell family had gone from accepting a tithing from the settlement six months before the incident in the sixteenth century to murdering everyone living there. After hundreds of years of getting along peacefully, did Lord Cabell just wake up one morning and decide to torch all his tenants? It wasn't as if he did anything with the land afterward. Was it purely religious fervor or had something else happened?

The thought was playing through my mind as my eyes slowly drifted closed. I could ask Lord Cabell in the morning. Maybe he would know something more.

I must have fallen asleep then because the clock in the library had just struck three when I woke. Harper was sprawled haphazardly on the chair, her pretty dress heaved in every direction, arms and legs flung out, her mouth open wide.

As I came around, I realized the time. I was just rising, digging my pistol out of my dress pocket, when I heard the first tell-tale yowl outside.

Casting a glance at Harper, who looked like she would sleep through a dirigible air assault, I left her there then headed toward the back of the house.

Everything was so silent save the howl across the fen.

I worked my way through the house once more, digging my night goggles from my bag and slipping them on as I went. I cursed the stupid dress I was still wearing. Why hadn't I gone up to change?

I pushed through the ballroom, which was even more decorated than it had been the night before. The empty, dark eyes of the jack-o-lanterns stared out at me. I slipped out the back door and onto the garden terrace just as the creature howled once more. This time, it was definitely in the garden itself.

I pulled my weapon, adjusted my goggles, and began to move slowly through the mist into the elaborate garden. It was unearthly silent. Not a frog croaked nor a night bird called. Everything in the heavy mist was still. Whatever was out here with me was moving slowly, hunting. I scanned around, letting my mooneye do the hard work. Once again, I spotted apparitions in the mist, spirits appearing then disappearing. Some moved through the dense air back toward the house, others passed by then faded to nothing, mere wisps. The palms of my hands and bottoms of my feet tingled.

Deep in the garden, I heard a low growl.

I followed the sound, and for the briefest of moments, spotted the flash of ruby red eyes.

Werewolf.

"Come along now," I called lightly. "A bit rude to be skulking around like this. Why don't you come out, and let's have a chat. I came all the way from London to see what you were about, after all." I waited for any reply, but there was none. I felt the eyes of the beast on me. I had to remind myself that I was not in London anymore. While the werewolves I knew were refined enough to teach at a college, it didn't mean a rustic wolf would be anything of the sort. Hell, out here, maybe the creature was as lawless and wild as werewolf packs had been in the past.

I pulled my knife and readied it, my pistol in my other hand.

Well, if whoever it was didn't want to come along quietly, there was always another way to handle this problem.

"Agent Louvel?" a voice called from the veranda.

Lord Cabell.

The bushes not far from me rustled, the mist swirling in a quick movement.

"Agent Louvel?" Lord Cabell called once more.

"Hell's bells," I whispered then raced toward the house. "Edison, go back inside. Edison, go inside now!" I shouted through the mist.

Racing quickly, I pushed past the statues of the stony-eyed angels. Under the light of the nearly full moon, I could just make out the silhouette of Lord Cabell standing at the rail of the terrace looking over the garden. And then I spotted a dark shape moving toward him—fast.

I aimed and fired.

The sound of the gunshot echoed loudly through the night.

The creature slid to a stop. It turned and looked back at me, red eyes blaring. I could barely make out its shape, but something about the beast looked different. The shape of its ears or size... I wasn't sure what, but something was off.

"Come on," I said, calling it in. "Come to me now."

The monster snarled at me then turned and rushed toward the house.

"Edison, go inside now!" I screamed through the mist.

The werewolf and I rushed toward the veranda.

Instead of listening to me, Lord Cabell stepped into the garden.

"Agent Louvel?" he called.

"Dammit," I whispered, pushing myself hard.

I was going to make it. I was going to make it.

I saw red eyes flash as the creature wove around the statues, approaching Lord Cabell on his left flank.

I raced up the steps.

"Agent Louvel," Edison said, moving toward me.

I heard a low growl then turned in time to see the monster rushing toward us. Its body was still partially hidden by the mist, but the glowing red eyes told the tale.

I pulled my knife, grabbed Edison, and thrust him behind me. I readied myself.

At that same moment, the door to the ballroom opened, and Harper appeared.

"Holy shit," she said, taking in the situation.

Lifting her gun, she fired. The wolf had just a split second to anticipate the shot before leaping off the balcony and out of sight.

Without delay, Harper turned and rushed after the werewolf.

"What was that?" Edison whispered. "Was that a hellhound?"

"Close. Now, would you kindly go back inside," I

said. "I need to help Harper find that thing before it gets away."

"W-what was that?"

"Inside, Lord Cabell. Now."

He stared out into the mist. "Right," he said then finally headed back inside.

I turned and ran after Harper.

On the far side of the garden, the wolf let off a low howl. He was retreating to the fen.

"Oh no you don't." I raced in the direction of the sound.

I was startled by the sound of a gunshot. Then another.

"Harper," I called, my stomach tying into a knot of worry.

I reached the edge of the garden to find Harper there, her pistol poised before her, glaring toward the misty treeline.

"There," she whispered, pointing. "I missed—stupid rummy head—but the wolf is just there. Look."

I followed her gaze. On the other side of the trees, back out in the fen, I spotted the telltale red eyes.

The creature growled.

"He's luring us," I whispered, well aware that the beast would hear me if I spoke too loudly.

The wolf turned then loped out of sight, back into the mist.

"Right," Harper said.

"Well, at least we've one advantage. We know where he's headed," I said.

Harper lifted a finger. "Sorry about this," she said then turned and gripped the trunk of a nearby tree. A second later, she vomited violently and loudly.

I shook my head then stepped toward the fen.

"Oh my god," Harper whispered after a moment.

I pulled a handkerchief from my pocket and handed it to Harper. "Here," I said, patting her on the back, which only made her vomit again.

After a moment, she said, "Don't tell Agent Hunter. Promise me," Harper said. "I'd die of embarrassment."

I chuckled. "I won't, but you need to head back to the house and see to Lord Cabell."

"And where are you going?"

I cast my eyes back out on the moor. "Out there."

CHAPTER 15
Of Romans and Druids

Retracing the path we had taken with Mister Aaron, I headed out the back gate and onto the road. At three in the morning. In a bank of fog. Chasing a werewolf who did not appear to be entirely friendly. Or dapper. Or charming. And probably didn't smirk.

I thought about slipping my night optics on but knew their green glow would give me away in the darkness. Relying on the dim light of the moon penetrating the mist, I headed out onto the moor.

My heart beat hard as I made my way, listening to every rustle in the brush, feeling the world around me with my senses. Working in the city was one thing but working in the country was quite another. I was used to the occasional tart popping out of an alley or a thief thinking he could make a go for my pockets, but a bolting deer or a rustling bunny somehow sounded just as deadly when you couldn't actually see what was out there—knowing still that something in the mist wanted to kill you.

As I walked, I felt the presence of the otherworld swimming around me. There was something heavy in the air, a strange sort of energy I had never encountered before. For the briefest of moments, I felt confused, lost. Part of me wanted to turn back. There were strange, ethereal voices in the mist whispering to me.

"It's here."
"Turn here."
"Turn now."
"Come."
"Too far."
"Go back."
"Turn left."
"Turn right."

I couldn't tell if the voices were speaking aloud or if I heard them in my own head. But what I did know was that strange power that lived inside me resisted their instruction. The deep, secret thing within me kept my feet firmly on a steady path forward. Yet the further I walked from Cabell Manor, the more the whispers spoke, giving me repeated and contradicting instructions.

I paused a moment in the swirling mist and gazed

around me. The shadowy fingers of dead trees were silhouetted in the moonlight. Everything had an eerie bluish glow. From somewhere across the fen, a creature barked—a fox? Its strange voice reverberated through the mist.

Maybe this was a bad idea.

It wasn't that I was frightened, but there was something happening here I didn't understand. My skin had risen in gooseflesh, my palms and feet tingling. The magic here was so heavy, so thick, I could almost taste it.

"Go back," a voice said. This time, however, the voice did not hold the same ghostly quality. It was firm and strong.

I turned and watched as a woman in a long robe, her face mostly hooded, appeared from through the fog. She walked with a tall, hooked staff. She had a strange silvery glow about her. All the hair on the top of my head rose, and a shiver snaked through my body. As the woman drew closer, I realized I could not hear the sound of her footfalls. The mist parted before her.

I lifted my gun and aimed at her.

"Go back, Agent Louvel."

"Who are you?"

"No one. But you must go back. It is only that light living inside you that is keeping you safe from the whispers on the wind. The heavy magic here is intended to confuse. It's working its charms on you. For the moment, it's failing. But only for the moment."

"Confuse me? Why?"

She chuckled lightly. "It's nothing personal. The charms are meant to confuse anyone, really. But they were originally intended for the Romans."

"The Romans."

"An enchantment was set on this fen to hide it and the settlement from the Romans. The ancient magic users are long gone, but the spell still holds. No one roams these fens at night and leaves unscathed."

"Yet here we are," I said, eyeing her closely with my mooneye.

I didn't know who this woman was, but one thing was sure, she wasn't human. My good eye saw the glow around her, but my mooneye saw more. She wasn't solid. Her body appeared opalescent, light and color swirling like water in the form of a body. The disparity between the images confused my mind and made my head hurt.

"I am always here," she said lightly. "But you should not be. What you seek is not what you think. Return to the ruins tomorrow before dusk. I will help you."

"Why?"

"Because I know what you do not."

"And the wolf?"

"Come tomorrow, Agent Louvel. But go back now

before the old whispers overpower that spark within you," she said then stepped back into the mist.

A moment later, I heard a strange wooshing sound, and a blast of air moved around me.

She was gone.

My hands trembled.

I looked out across the moor.

"Hell's bells," I whispered, debating what to do.

With a shake of the head, I turned and headed back toward Cabell Manor.

The spark within you.

And just what in the hell *is* that spark?

I RETURNED TO THE MANOR TO FIND HARPER IN THE SMALL library with Lord Cabell. She looked worried, pale, and tired. Lord Cabell rose when I entered.

"Agent Louvel. Thank goodness."

"Clem, are you all right?" Harper asked.

I nodded. "And you? Lord Cabell, are you okay?"

"Rattled, but unharmed, thanks to the two of you."

"Did you find anything?" Harper asked.

Yes. Definitely.

I shook my head. "No. The mist was too dense, and the beast was gone. Tomorrow, Harper and I will return to the ruins."

Edison frowned, slugged back a drink, then poured himself another. "If we can't resolve this matter, I will have to cancel the ball. Charlotte will not be pleased."

I looked at Harper who was pushing her fingertips into her temple. Lord Cabell had nearly been mauled by a werewolf, but the ball was the first thing on his mind. *Priorities, people!*

"Why don't you head back to bed," I suggested. "I believe the worst of the danger has passed."

"Did you get a look at the beast, Agent?" Lord Cabell asked. "I'm afraid it happened so quickly that it was just a passing blur for me."

"Briefly."

"And?"

"Agent Hunter was right to send us here."

"Damn," Lord Cabell said. "You know, I never quite believed in the family curse. But now…"

Lord Cabell glanced at Harper. "I say, Agent Harper, are you unwell?"

"Oh, just a bit of a headache," she said.

"All right, let me go up," Lord Cabell said, slogging back his drink. "I can't believe Charlotte didn't wake with all this ruckus."

"Mister Frances was here," Harper told me. "The servants were worried."

I nodded. "It should be calm now."

Harper raised a questioning eyebrow at me but asked nothing more.

"I'm headed into the village after breakfast," Lord Cabell said. "That's enough excitement for one night. If you think it's safe now, I'll turn in."

"Yes, I do," I replied.

"Very well. Goodnight, Agents," he said then turned and headed out of the library.

After he had gone, Harper slowly lifted herself out of the chair.

"Come on, rummy," I told her. "Let's get you to bed."

"What did you find out there?"

"Not the werewolf. He was long gone. But I did wander into an ancient spell set by the druids to confuse the Romans."

"Wait, what? The Romans? How do you know that?"

"Because a woman living in the moor told me so."

"A woman?"

"I'm not entirely sure she was human."

"A spirit then?"

"Maybe."

"Maybe? A witch?"

"Honestly, I really don't know. But she asked me to return to the ruins at dusk tomorrow night."

"She probably wants to sacrifice you on that altar."

"Could be. But that's a very morbid take on the matter, Elaine."

"You have no idea what I saw in Egypt."

"I'm beginning to get the picture. Now, let's get you to bed," I said, taking her by the arm.

Harper gave me a half-hearted laugh, and we headed upstairs.

CHAPTER 16

A Pinch of Practical Magic

I'd only gotten a few hours of sleep when the sounds of voices rising up from outside the manor woke me. Frances was speaking to the wagon driver. I could just catch their voices on the breeze. Frances told the driver that Lord Cabell wanted to leave within half an hour. Dizzy with tiredness, I forced myself to get dressed.

I was almost ready when the maid, Emma, appeared. "Oh, Agent. You're already awake," she said in a half-whisper so as not to wake Harper. I didn't bother to tell her that she might need a trumpet to get Harper out of bed.

"I wanted to catch Lord Cabell before he left for the village. I'd like to ride along with him. Can you ask the driver to wait for me?"

"I'll let his Lordship's valet know right now," she

said then cast a glance at Harper whose mouth was open wide, drool pouring down her cheek.

The girl chuckled at Harper then slipped back out of the room.

I checked my weapons, reloading my pistol and slipping my knife on my belt. Pausing before the mirror, I cast a glance at myself. The gloom over Cabell Manor made me look paler than usual, and there were dark rings under my eyes. But I was getting close. The woman on the moor had told me that whatever I was hunting, it wasn't what I thought. Well, we'd see about that. Because if there was one thing I knew very well, it was werewolves.

I slipped out of the room and down the stairs to the foyer. There, I found Lady Charlotte and Lord Cabell waiting. They were speaking earnestly with one another. Lady Charlotte looked agitated—though very nicely dressed. Lord Cabell's countenance was like that of a drowning man.

"Ah, here is Agent Louvel," Lord Cabell said when he spotted me on the stairs. The expression on his face suggested I had just saved him from an unpleasant conversation.

Lady Charlotte frowned off in the distance then turned to me and smiled. "Good morning, Agent. It appears I missed the excitement last night. After working all day on the ball preparations, I'm afraid a hurricane could have passed through here, and I would have missed it entirely."

"I'm just glad to see your Ladyship safe and sound," I said, forcing a smile.

She gave me half a nod and forced a smile herself.

Good, at least our dislike of one another was mutual.

"My valet tells me you'd like to come into the village," Lord Cabell said.

"If possible, yes."

"Do you think there is a connection with something in the village?"

"You never know. I just wanted a look around, if it's all right."

"Of course. I was just about to head out if you're ready."

"But Agent Louvel hasn't had any breakfast," Lady Charlotte protested, scandalized by the idea.

"It's no matter. I'm rarely hungry first thing in the morning," I lied. My stomach was growling, but she didn't need to know that.

"Oh, very well then. Is Agent Harper awake?"

"Not yet."

"Very well, Agent. Edison, I'll see you when you return," she said then with a nod she left in the direction of the ballroom.

Lord Cabell motioned for me to follow him outside.

"Sorry about the wagon. I do have a steam-auto, but

I need to pick something up in the village, so the wagon makes more sense," he told me.

"It's fine," I replied.

Lord Edison nodded to the driver then got in the wagon, turning to offer me a hand up. Once I was settled in, we set off.

"My sister was rather vexed with me this morning. I warned her we might need to cancel the ball. She wants to wait. Apparently, me nearly getting mauled wasn't enough to convince her."

"I did notice the tension."

"I'd be disappointed if you didn't. My sister loves the ball. You see, Agent, she spends much of her time alone out here on the fen. I travel often, but I always try to come home to attend the event because it means so much to her. This event is her social highlight of the year. I hate to deprive her of it."

"I'm sure Harper and I will have the matter settled today."

"Really? That's a bold proclamation."

"Boldness is an affliction I suffer from in spades," I said with a grin.

Lord Cabell laughed. As he did so, however, his eyes raked my face once more. "Were you... No, I'm sorry. It's rude to ask."

My stomach knotted for a brief moment, but I let the feeling pass. "My eye?"

He nodded.

"I was involved in an incident more than a year ago."

"And a creature did that?"

"Yes."

"A creature like what I have here?"

"Yes, but my monster was a scoundrel. Weren't you, Fenton?" I said, patting the hide on my belt.

Lord Cabell paled, his mouth hanging open. He leaned in close to me. "It is true what Sir Edwin has told me, that there are beasts among us."

"Yes."

"And the curse on my family?"

"There is something in the fen, but I'm not sure that it is related to the curse. The fens are vast and unpopulated. It's a good place to hide. And your ruins are a great place to take cover. But I was wondering about something. Why did you go to the fen at night? It's so very dense and confusing out there. Why go?"

Lord Cabell shifted uncomfortably then said, "As I told you, I was checking the site for a new steam station. But to be honest, the time got away from me, and before I knew it, it was night. I hadn't intended to be out there after dark. I've walked the land for years as a boy, so I knew the way back. But I understand your meaning. The mists can be...confusing. But that night was different. That night, I got something's attention."

"I'm surprised you would consider the ruins a site for development. With the standing stones there, it's more a place to preserve. Your lands are rich with history."

"I came away with the same notion. It's a special place. It shouldn't be disturbed. Placing the station there was my sister's idea. She doesn't place the same value on the historical significance of the land or, as she called it, *sentimental notions*. Honestly, I assessed the land to end the discussion between us. I won't develop that land."

I smiled. "I'm glad to hear that."

Lord Cabell nodded. "But I would rather not have a monster roaming about all the same."

"I'm sure. Harper and I will handle it. Whatever vermin you have out there, it can't be any worse than he was," I said, tapping Fenton once more.

"Indeed. Though your scar has healed well," Lord Cabell said, eyeing my face again.

"It has."

"Can you—forgive my curiosity—can you see at all?"

"Yes. Differently, but I can still see. And the claw marks are much less obvious now."

Lord Cabell smiled sympathetically then pulled off his glove. He lifted his hand, pointing to the skin beside his pinkie finger where there was a long, dark scar. He flexed and unflexed his fingers, and when he did so, I noticed a strange misalignment in his grip.

"Your surgeon was better than my butcher, though he was the best money could buy," he said.

"What happened?"

"I was born with six fingers, as was Charlotte—but she'd be scandalized if anyone ever knew. When we were mere babies, the surgeon removed our sixth fingers. The sixth finger is hereditary to the Cabell family. My father once told me it's because we carry the blood of druids who once walked these lands, a physical symbol of the magic buried inside us," he said then chuckled. "That's the strange family story that won me the friendship of Sir Edwin at Eaton. What an odd, wonderful fellow he is," Lord Cabell said with a chuckle.

"How very true," I agreed, my mind momentarily going to thoughts of Edwin. Since I'd gotten here, I'd hardly had a chance to think of him, but the sound of his name warmed my heart. But as much as I wanted to ruminate on the idea of that fine man, the fact that the Cabell family line had the hallmark of six fingers settled heavily on my imagination. At once, I began to twist around theories.

"Are there any other Cabell family members living in the area, cousins or distant relatives?" I asked.

Lord Cabell shook his head. "No. Why?"

"Just considering possibilities."

"When she was living, the dowager used to live at Cabell Place, a house in the village. Since she died, we've lent it to the village council to use as a school. Otherwise, it's just Lady Charlotte and me."

"I see. So you really are all alone. You mentioned how lonely Charlotte is out here. Why doesn't she come to London? Isn't that what most fashionable ladies do?"

Lord Cabell smiled lightly. "She is lonely, but my sister is also a bit of an eccentric. I think the ball is enough action to fill her for a year at a time."

I chuckled, but his comment left me wondering how eccentric she might actually be.

It wasn't long before we arrived at the local village. The quaint little town rose out of the flat landscape, a tangle of buildings that were made of pale grey stone. The driver stopped the cart outside of a building that appeared to be some sort of workshop. There was a large sculpture hanging over the door. It depicted a scene of gnomes tinkering away at a mechanical man. The name of the shop, The Clockarium, was made of metal.

"Where are you headed, Agent?" Lord Cabell asked.

"Just a couple of errands to run."

"Good, good. I'll be within," he said, motioning to the workshop. "Let's say we meet at the pub, The Three Lions, in an hour? Should be lunchtime by then."

I hadn't taken Lord Cabell as one who'd rub shoulders with the locals, but I was glad to hear it. "Very well."

I slipped out of the wagon and headed into the village while Lord Cabell went into the workshop. Scanning the signs on the buildings, I hunted the apothecary. The little town was far busier than I expected. There was even an airship tower at the edge of town, but I didn't notice any airships in port. A bakery, millinery, grocer, post, bank, and other shops lined the street. I worked my way down the row until I spotted a sign boasting a blue mortar and pestle, the apothecary.

Giving my weapons a passing touch, ensuring all was in order, I headed toward the door, my palms and feet already tingling.

The sharp, tangy scents of the medicines burned my nose the moment I entered the place. Jars lined the walls. Bunches of dried herbs hung overhead. There was an elderly woman standing at the counter. On the other side, a woman with red hair pulled into a bun was explaining to her how to apply salve to her foot.

"Thank you, Shannon. Thank you, thank you," the old woman told the apothecary.

"Of course, Mrs. Johnson. Come back in a few days and let me know how you are."

"Thank you, my dear," the old woman said then slipped a jar into her basket and turned to leave.

When she spotted me, she gasped softly.

I stepped aside, allowing the woman to pass by. The bell above the door rang as the woman headed out. Through the window, I saw her pass a suspicious glance back at the door.

"Funny how she doesn't mind the witch, but the werewolf hunter spooked her," the woman at the counter said.

I looked at the apothecary. She was leaning against a post, her hands in the pockets of her apron. She gave me a wry smile.

"Never know what will spook them," I said.

So, she already knew who I was, and she wasn't hiding what she was. That was a good way to start.

"I suppose seeing you is enough to raise the red flag of warning, Agent Louvel."

"Well, I don't mean to alarm anyone. So, it appears you know who I am."

"I do. My daughter, Kerry, told me you were at the manor. I'm Shannon Millhouse. Apothecary."

"And witch."

"Yes, that too. But I'm a hearth witch, Agent. No black magic practiced here. Now, if you need a good foot ointment…" she said, motioning around the shop.

Most of the witches I encountered in London practiced black magic, dark witchcraft. I seldom came across a white witch, though I knew of them and their earthy, healing magic. In many ways, they were akin to druids, but I didn't know enough about either to be able to differentiate.

"I see."

"So, Agent Louvel, what can I do for you?"

"Since you don't need smiting, do you have anything for a headache?"

She raised an eyebrow at me. "Are you ill?"

I shook my head. "For a friend. Partook in too much wine, I'm afraid."

She chuckled, turned back to her shelves, and got to work opening jars and mixing ingredients. "So, you are here to save the Cabell family from the curse."

"I believe I am here to save the All Hallows Ball from being canceled and prevent Lady Charlotte from feeling disappointed."

At that, she laughed out loud. "May the Mother Goddess forbid. I see Lady Charlotte makes the same impression upon people everywhere she goes."

"How does your daughter like working at the manor? I'm surprised you don't have her apprenticing with you," I asked leadingly.

"She wasn't interested. She has magic in her hands, but her interest is in food. I sent her to the big house to learn about service and cooking because it was her wish."

"You don't mind her working for a family cursed by witches?"

Reaching for another jar, she paused. After a moment, she set it on the counter then turned to me. "Witches is a misnomer, as you no doubt already realized."

"Druids then."

"Not even that. You forget that at one time, all the people in this land were pagan. All the people in this land once worshipped the old gods and practiced the old ways."

"I see," I said, truly grateful to the woman for putting some pieces of the puzzle together. Old Lord Cabell hadn't murdered witches; he had wiped out a village that clung to the old ways. At the beating heart of England was a pantheon of gods, of old, sacred things and pagan ways that didn't want to be forgotten. The Cabell family had been cursed for trying to extinguish one of the last strongholds of the old gods. "What do you make of the curse? Can such a thing be lifted, mended by time or the actions of later generations?"

She shrugged. "It depends on the actions and understanding of later generations. Perhaps Lord Edison Cabell is capable of making amends, his sister—for all her professed interest in the occult—is not.

"Did you know that there is something awake in the fens?"

The woman smiled knowingly. "Indeed, I do. But I'm not sure we're talking about the same thing," she said then turned back to her mortar. Giving the powder one last grind, she poured the concoction into a paper pouch, sealed it, then handed it to me. "Two teaspoons mixed with water every four hours until the symptoms go away."

"Thank you," I said, taking it from her. "What do I owe you?"

"Nothing. But leave my daughter in peace. She doesn't know anything, and you've scared my girl out of her wits. I reassured her that you're just doing your job, that people like you are trained to notice people like us. I told her that she doesn't need to be afraid. Does she?"

"Not of me. I'm sorry she was frightened."

Shannon inclined her head to me in thanks. "Once this matter at Cabell Manor is settled, you'll be going?"

"Yes. I have no interest in terrorizing the local, friendly hearth witch."

She chuckled. "What more can I ask for? You'll be going back to the ruins, back out on the fen?"

"Yes. Whatever is lurking out there, I need to find it before someone gets hurt."

She nodded, took a deep breath, then said, "A word of warning. This is an old place, a magical place. There are things out there you will not have encountered before, creatures who are just trying to survive. It would not be wise to push them."

"What kind of creatures?"

"I—" she said then cast a glance toward the window.

I followed her gaze. To my surprise, the sky had suddenly become overcast, and rain had started to fall. Raindrops splattered on the window of the shop.

"I dare not say more. Tread carefully, and be...reverent."

I raised an eyebrow at her.

She inclined her head. "Blessed be ye."

I gave the packet a little wave, slipped it into my pocket, then headed outside. In the distance, thunder rolled, but the rain stopped. A moment later, the sun shone through the clouds once more.

Reverent.

Now, I didn't hear that word every day. The fens were turning out to be far more interesting than I ever expected.

CHAPTER 17
Of Lions and Gargoyles

I walked the length of the village, passing the church Lord Samson had mentioned—and its mildly pagan stones—, the Cabell House school, and other small cottages and businesses. Aside from the apothecary, nothing else stuck out. Perplexed by Shannon's words, I headed to The Three Lions where I found Lord Cabell surrounded by a group of local villagers, laughing loudly and looking far more at ease than I had seen him since I'd arrived.

"Agent Louvel," he called when I entered.

The others gave me a less friendly welcome, eyeing me and my red cape suspiciously.

Lord Cabell waved me over. "Gents, this is the lady I was telling you about."

Oh lord.

I smiled at the little assembly. "Gentlemen."

They eyed me over, unsure of how to respond. A couple of men tipped their hats. The others simply stared, looking me over from head to toe.

"Let's get a drink for the agent," Lord Cabell said then motioned to the bartender to pour me a bitter. Lord Cabell retrieved the cup, handed it to me, then clicked his glass against mine.

"To better days," he said.

"To better days," I agreed.

Lord Cabell drank deeply.

Mindful of my words to Harper, I took a small sip.

"And what is it, again, the agent does?" one of the local men asked.

"Law enforcement," I said with a wry grin.

"So you're a lady constable?" one of the gentlemen asked. He swayed as he spoke, the front of his shirt wet with either ale or perspiration, I wasn't sure which. He eyed my pistols.

"Something like that."

"Very modern," one of the men said, the others nodding vigorously in agreement.

I tried not to roll my eyes.

"Let's have a seat, Agent," Lord Cabell said, motioning to a table in the back. "I'm hungry. You?"

"Very."

Lord Cabell clapped the men around us on the backs, shook hands with the lot, then waved for me to follow him to a table at the corner. He motioned to the bartender then settled back into his seat with his drink.

"Find what you were after?" Lord Cabell asked.

"In a way. And you?"

"Oh, you'll see," he said with a grin. "I can't wait to hear what you think. Now, you need to tell me something about yourself. How long have you worked with Sir Edwin?"

"A bit over a year."

"He spoke very highly of you," Lord Cabell said, a glimmer in his eye. "Very highly."

"Did he, now?"

"He let me know you'd be staying on for the ball, assuming all goes well, as his guest."

I lifted my drink and sipped, quieting the butterflies that had suddenly swarmed my stomach. "Yes. Well, Edwin and I are attached."

"So he mentioned, but I didn't want to bring it up in front of Charlotte. Poor dear, she had her heart set on Edwin for some time. I warned her it would all come to nothing."

"And now?"

"Ah, that's all past. There's a Scottish lord with a slightly less foggy estate at whom she's now set her cap."

I chuckled. "And you, Lord Cabell, has some young lady set her cap at you and your foggy estate?"

"Several, but none quite as endearing as Agent Harper. Do you mind my asking about her?"

I coughed lightly, choking a little on my ale. "Harper?"

"Yes. Is Agent Harper attached?"

The tapster returned with two more drinks and two plowman's platters. My mouth started watering as soon as I spotted the Scotch egg. I was famished. But I was also intrigued. In her drunken state last night, had Harper managed to land herself a lord?

"I'm not certain, honestly," I said, thinking of Harper's history with Alan Quartermain. But she was here, and he was in Africa. I didn't know what, exactly, that meant. I suspected that whatever had flourished between them was now done and over with. But I wasn't sure.

"She's such a bright thing, and she seems like a sincere girl."

"So she is."

"I grow tired of courtly ladies and their games. I've had enough guile for one lifetime. I suspect Edwin shares my sentiments on the matter. Do you know anything about Agent Harper's family?"

And here is where his hopes come to die. "Only a little. Harper is a commoner, like me."

Lord Cabell waved his hand dismissively. "None of that matters these days." Lord Cabell picked up his tankard once more, grinning as he sipped, lost in his thoughts.

Good for Harper.

Well, maybe good for Harper. I suppose that depended on what she was looking for. And honestly, I had no idea.

I turned back to my platter once more, breaking off bits of cheese, Scotch egg, and greens until I had formed the perfect bite. Sticking the delicious morsels in my mouth, I sighed contentedly then gave Lord Cabell a passing look. He was staring off into the distance, a silly grin on his face.

I chuckled. I wonder if Harper knew she's been on a big game hunt all this time. Sometimes love sneaks up on you like that. One day you're just doing your job, the next you realize your heart has run out the door.

Lifting my tankard, I took a sip, my eyes scanning the tavern. They came to rest on the image on the wall directly across from me. It was a painting of a lion. I drank once more, trying to drown the sinking feeling in my stomach.

Yes, sometimes your heart runs off before you even know it.

Bloody traitor.

After Lord Cabell and I finished our lunches, we headed back outside where I found the wagon waiting. There were two very strange lumps covered with a tarp in the back of the cart.

"Shopping?" I asked Lord Cabell.

"It's a surprise. I'll show you when we get back."

We slipped into the wagon and headed back toward the house. Lord Cabell, who was about three tankards too deep, chatted all the while. He pointed out every spot in the landscape, told me about his grandmother, asked me about Harper's family again—which made me decidedly uneasy—and left me with the impression that he had not yet decided how he was planning to approach Agent Harper on the subject of his sudden crush.

When we arrived at Cabell Manor, Lord Cabell instructed the driver to pull the wagon around to the garden in the back. I slipped out of the wagon while Lord Cabell climbed into the back.

"Well, Agent Louvel. Let's see what you think of these," he said, untying the tarp to reveal...sculptures.

"What are those?" I asked.

The wagon driver climbed into the back, and together, the two men wrestled the first of the heavy metal sculptures to the ground. Lord Cabell stood back, his hands on his hips, and looked down at the creation.

"That, Agent Louvel, is a gargoyle. A clockwork gargoyle," he said then bent to tinker with the machine.

I stared at the mechanism. He was right. It was a beast made of clockwork with wings like a bat and the face of a gargoyle just like those sitting all along the rooftop of Cabell Manor.

Lord Cabell labored on a panel underneath the first creature, and a moment later, its eyes flashed blue. The mech turned its head, flapped its metal wings, and stretched its limbs. I heard the sound of the clockwork mechanisms turning, almost like the tick of a clock, as the creation sprang to life.

"It's a security feature. I need to place some sensors around the garden then it will patrol the grounds for us, alerting us of any intruders. It's equipped with a sound box, ethics boards, an aether core, Hawking optics, all the best."

"That's impressive."

"I bought two," he said, slipping back into the wagon.

"Then I'm doubly impressed," I said, kneeling down to look at the amazing creation.

"Impressed with what, Agent?" a voice asked from behind me.

Lady Charlotte.

"My clockwork gargoyles," Lord Cabell said as he

and the wagon driver lowered the second clockwork creature.

"God, how garish. They're perfect," Lady Charlotte said with a laugh. "What do they do?"

"They're security. They'll patrol the garden."

"You must ensure they can be seen during the ball. That will give people a fright. How horrifying they are. I love them."

I raised an eyebrow at Lady Charlotte. She might not have been a bad match for Edwin after all. Though I suspected having to scrub Phillip Phillips from her knickers was probably beyond her limit of tolerance.

Lord Cabell tugged on a large wooden crate, pulling it down from the back of the wagon. "I need to configure them a bit. Right now, they are on standby. The man explained what to do. I'll need to set them so they don't start shrieking at the sight of the gardeners. They've been tinkered to respond to a password."

"Pray tell, what is it?" Lady Charlotte asked.

Lord Cabell chuckled. "Heel. Sorry, not very creative, I know. They will respond to a variety of commands. Once I have them up and running, I'll go over all the commands with you."

"I love them. Thank you, Edison."

"Of course. No doubt Agent Louvel and Agent Harper will have the matter here settled in no time, but considering something tried to kill me last night, the idea of extra security was very appealing."

Lady Charlotte glanced at me. "Indeed. My brother tells me you put yourself between him and whatever was prowling around the garden. Very brave, Agent. I was...pleased to hear."

And surprised, by her tone.

"That's my job. Speaking of which, I should see how Agent Harper is coming along."

"She's in the small library."

Of course she's in the small *library.*

"Thank you," I told Lady Charlotte then turned to Lord Cabell. "Thank you for letting me ride along with you."

"My pleasure," he said with a wave. A screwdriver in hand, he bent to look at the gargoyle once more, completely distracted by his new toy. To my surprise, Lady Charlotte also bent to have a closer look.

Leaving the two alone to play with mechanical monsters, I headed inside. Harper and I had monsters of our own to chase. I slipped the packet the apothecary had given me out of my vest pocket. If Harper and I were going to be hunting monsters on the fen, while being *reverent*, something told me that Harper was going to need this.

CHAPTER 18
Reading Between the Lines

"Reverent?" Harper asked then paused to polish off the last of the medicinal tonic. "That's... I'm confused. Are you sure that's what she said?"

"Yes, I'm sure."

"What—or who the hell—is out there?" Harper asked then picked up her cup and examined it. There was sandy sediment at the bottom. "You're sure she seemed all right? I mean, for all we know, she could have given you poison."

"Well, you've drunk it now, so I guess we'll see."

"Very funny," Harper said then picked up her teacup, which she had loaded with sugar, to wash down the medicine.

"She was a hearth witch. A white witch. My eye told me she was fine."

"Well—and no offense to your eye—but I hope you're right. God. Never, ever let me drink wine again."

I chuckled. "It happens to the best of us."

"So you said. Do I have a vague recollection of you mentioning something about a brawny Scottish tapster? Did this happen to you in Edinburgh?"

"What? No. Of course not. That's not what I said. I was airsick in Scotland," I said with a wink. "Now, what have you uncovered?"

"I see you're changing the subject. Clem, that woman you met on the fen, the one who told you to come back tonight—was she… What was she?"

"I don't know, to be honest. She wasn't a werewolf. And she was definitely a magic user of some kind. But… Well, I don't know."

"But what?"

"Well, I know you don't trust my all-seeing evil eye, but when I looked at her, she looked like…water."

"A spirit?"

I shook my head. "They look like shadows."

Harper frowned. "Water."

I shrugged.

"Okay, well, I don't know what she is, but Lord Samson's musings about some wandering ruffians got me curious. The library didn't store back copies of the local newspaper, but to our luck, the servants store the newspapers to use for packing or tidying up. I spent an hour in a dusty room with Missus Carroll, who is very talkative, by the way, and I came up with these," she said, handing me a pile of clippings.

I flipped through the papers. There was a public warning about some vagrants being spotted in the country, an article on a scuffle in which a local constable was severely wounded, and another article about a robbery that took place on the road between the Samson and Cabell estates. There was nothing supernatural mentioned in the reports, but still. The behavior smacked of a werewolf pack.

"And, Missus Carroll, who had no respect for my headache as she chatted on, also let slip that the vagabonds mentioned in the article were seen lingering around Cabell Manor. Once, or so she told me, they came to the house begging alms."

"Missus Carroll spoke to them?"

Harper shook her head. "She didn't, but Lady Charlotte did."

"Wait, didn't Lady Charlotte say that the vagrants hadn't been seen here?"

"That's what she said."

"Why lie?"

Harper shrugged. "Maybe she didn't want to worry Lord Cabell. Missus Carroll said Lord Cabell was away at the time."

I frowned.

"And what about you? Discover anything besides white witches?"

"Indeed, I did. A couple of interesting things, actually. First, Lord Cabell and Miss Charlotte were both born with six fingers."

Harper turned to me. "No way."

"That's not all."

"That's plenty."

"And second, Lord Cabell asked me if you're attached to anyone."

At that, Harper's peaches and cream cheeks faded to alabaster white. "He what?"

"You heard me."

"What did you say?"

"That I wasn't sure."

"Clemeny!"

"Well, I'm not sure. There is Agent Quartermain—"

"No. Alan and I," Harper began then paused. "Agent Quartermain has found someone else abroad," she said, her voice catching at the end. "So, no."

"Oh, Harper. I'm sorry."

She shook her head. "No. It's all right. It's to be expected."

"I'll be sure to let Lord Cabell know the path is clear."

"You'll do no such thing."

"Won't I?"

"No. Please, no."

"What? Why not?"

"He's a Lord. And his sister is...well, I don't think she'd approve of someone like me. I don't want to deal with that."

"Lady Charlotte strikes me as the kind of lady who doesn't approve of anyone but herself. What about Lord Cabell? He seems nice enough."

"He's too tall."

"Really, Harper."

"And he's blond."

"What's the problem with that?"

"Nothing. It's just... Well, you have a propensity for blond men. I don't. I like men with dark hair."

"Really?"

"Cabell Manor is gloomy."

"So you don't like his enormous mansion?"

"No, it's just... Can we stop talking about this and go back to the case?"

"I'm just checking. I mean, if you don't like rich, handsome, and nice lords, I guess that's your business."

"Clemeny, I swear to god, I'd punch you in the face if I didn't have a headache. I'm not ready. Alan's news...surprised me. Now, back to the six-finger business. It could be a coincidence, you know."

"Could be. But probably not. Sorry, Harper. Don't punch me."

"I won't. And thanks."

"So, we have a formally six-fingered lord and lady and a monster with six fingers on the moor," I said.

"Family connection?" Harper mused.

"Lady Charlotte secretly going savage at night? Be a shame to have to put some silver irons on her."

"Oh, yes, I see you're really broken up about the idea," Harper said with a chuckle.

I grinned. "The Cabell's have old blood in them. A sixth finger is always a tell-tale sign of magic. We need to be watchful though. Something is happening just under the surface here."

"Isn't it always?"

My mind drifted to Lionheart once more. "Yes."

"Now what?"

"Now," I said, pulling out my pocket watch. "Now, it's three o'clock, and *I* am headed back out onto the fen. *You* will pay Lord Cabell a visit. Go check out that interesting but creepy clockwork gargoyles he purchased to patrol the property."

"Wait, what do you mean *you're* going back to the fen? I'm coming with you."

"No, you aren't. Someone must stay here to keep the Cabells safe, a job the gargoyles can't accomplish."

"But Clemeny, something could happen to you out there."

"Probably, but if I die, all that stands between Lord

Cabell and the werewolf is you and a bunch of cogs and gears. So you stay here."

Harper sighed. "You have all the fun."

"Oh, yes. It will be so much fun chasing monsters in an enchanted mist. You hear voices, see shapes. Lot's of fun. Still want to come?"

"Nope."

"Good. You stay for dinner and small talk, and I'll go talk to the lady made of water."

"And be reverent."

"Right, and be reverent."

"I don't like it. You need to be careful."

"Of course," I said then headed toward the door.

"I mean it. Edwin would never forgive me if something happened to you. And I couldn't live with myself either," Harper called.

"I'll be fine, Harper."

"Lionheart wouldn't forgive me either," she added.

I paused, my hand on the door handle. "Lionheart is gone."

Harper was silent for a moment. "He'll be back."

I didn't look at her. How in the name of God had she guessed?

"We'll see," I said then headed outside.

We'll see.

CHAPTER 19
Reverent

Carrying nearly every weapon I owned, I sneaked through the garden, trying to avoid the clockwork gargoyles that were not, apparently, on patrol just yet and headed back onto the fen.

I walked quickly, one eye on the sun. The fen was quiet save the call of birds, croaking frogs, and the distant sound of the windmills or hiss from steam stations. High overhead, an airship passed. It looked like it was headed toward the nearby town. As I walked, I tumbled all the pieces around in my mind. The vagrants. The witch. The stones. The wolf. The Cabell family with their six fingers. The woman in the moors. It was very possible that I was walking into a trap. The white witch had cautioned me. But why should I believe her over anyone else? But still, wasn't I usually more careful than this?

No.

Not at all.

I followed my instincts, which is why I *usually* got what I was after.

A fleeting image of Lionheart passed through my mind, his wistful smile playing on his lips while he gazed at me from across that table at the pub, all the while reminiscing about his son.

I *usually* got what I was after.

But not always.

The late afternoon sun was already sinking toward the horizon. I turned off the main road and walked toward the ruins. The autumn sky was lit up with soft colors. Dark amber and royal purple trimmed the skyline as the sun dipped out of sight. As I climbed the rise toward the village ruins, my mooneye spotted a soft blue glow around the standing stones. The otherworldly light outlined the ogham images carved on the menhirs. Something that looked like fireflies—except they were blue—darted all around the place. Every hair on my head rose, and my hands and feet tingled.

What in the world?

I took a deep breath, pulled my silver dagger, and cast a glance around. I could feel the energy of others not far away. I was definitely not alone. And there were more people here than just the woman. I felt many eyes on me.

Stepping carefully, I passed the stones and headed up the slope. When I neared the ruins, I smelled the soft scent of smoke in the air. As I crested the rise, I saw that the fire at the village center had been reignited. I turned around and gazed across the horizon. Fog rolled across the fen. It slithered down the road from the ruins and moved across the land, blanketing it in thick mist. It moved and turned as if guided by hand. Soon, the fog enveloped the ground below the ruins.

The enchantment had awoken, shielding the place from the Romans.

Or whatever else might saunter by.

As I stared in amazement, I caught the soft sound of singing.

I looked about but didn't see anyone.

Pulling my pistol, I followed the sound.

I knew where it was coming from.

I walked slowly through the ruins, my senses alert for even the slightest of movements.

I was very glad Mister Aaron had shot that damned pheasant. God knows if I didn't keep my wits about me, I was going to shoot the very next thing I saw. I crossed the space to the far side. There, I found the road that led to the ring of stones in the fens.

Taking a deep breath, I made my way slowly down the rise toward the stones.

As I neared, I realized I was right.

I wasn't alone.

Five figures stood inside the stones. All of them turned to look at me.

And not one of them was human.

I recognized the woman I had met in the mist. She wore the same robe, but in the dying light, I realized it was more blue than black. And the colors on her gown seemed to move. No. Not the colors. Her. She was vaguely translucent, as were the two other women and two men with her.

"Welcome, Clemeny Louvel," she called. I saw her mouth move, saw her say the words, but I realized I'd also heard her voice inside my head.

"Who are you?" I asked.

The woman stepped toward me.

I studied her and the others carefully. There was no red nor silver gleam in their eyes. They were not werewolves or vampires. But they were not human either. Narrowing my eyes, I studied each one, realizing their forms shivered, almost as if they were shifting in and out of this world.

"You're asking the wrong question," the tall man in the back said.

I gazed at him. He wore a heavy green robe. His face was shadowed by his hood. Like the woman, there was a translucence to him. But the energy that swirled around him, within him, was all green.

"*What* are you?" I asked.

Another of the women smiled. She was petite, and her robe was red like mine. But unlike my red cape, her dark red robe sparkled along the hem. "Now you're close to the right question. What *were* we is the better way to put it."

"We *still* are," the second man, a tall, lanky creature in a dark brown robe, said, correcting the petite woman.

"Yes, but barely," she said with an exasperated sigh.

"We are elementals, Clemeny Louvel. At least, that is how you will best understand us," the woman I had met in the mist told me. "Once, we were more. I was Afwyn, of the spring waters of the fens," she said then turned to the others. "Cad of the brambles, Elswyth of the marsh birds, Aife of the village hearth, Odgaddeau of the willows."

Reverent.

Reverent.

These were—are—gods. These were the gods of the Celts, nature spirits, local gods, gods who barely existed in our world as little more than elementals. No wonder they were translucent. They were fading from this world.

My hands shook.

Holstering my pistol, I knelt on one knee.

Afwyn chuckled softly. "I told you," she said to the others. "Can't you see the blood inside her?"

"But she knows nothing."

"For now."

"Rise, Clemeny Louvel."

I rose. Moving carefully, I entered the ring. Afwyn motioned for me to join her at the altar. It was laid with candles, fruits, autumn gourds, vegetables, and flowers.

"The white witch and her coven have been here," Afwyn said, admiring the altar. "They are good to remember the old ways, to honor us. Her daughter brings offerings sometimes, as do the other witches in the village."

"So there is a coven here? Not just the witch and her daughter."

"Yes."

"And Lady Charlotte, is she part of that coven?"

Aife, the petite woman in the red robe, laughed. "No, Clemeny Louvel, she is a tourist and a burden."

She didn't have to tell me that.

But Aife was a goddess, so she could pretty much tell me anything she wanted.

I looked at Afwyn. In the dying light, I saw her

bright blue eyes swim and turn. Under the fading beams of sunlight, I saw the woman and saw through her all at once.

"You told me that I didn't really know what I was seeking. There is a werewolf on the moor. I was seeking the monster, and I found it. But I also found the five of you. I am…speechless to be in your presence, but what of the werewolf?"

Afwyn turned to the others.

They looked at one another. Elswyth, the eldest in appearance and wearing a pale pink robe, her head covered in a hood of feathers, stepped toward me.

"What have you discovered about werewolves in the fen?"

"I don't know. There was a pack here. The records seem to indicate that a rogue pack lived in this area for several years then moved on."

"So they did. Chased from Lord Samson's lands, the pack found a landowner who was sympathetic to and keenly interested in their plight. That landowner let them live amongst our ruins for a short space of time."

"Here? They lived here?" I said, looking back at the ruins. "The landowner—Lady Charlotte?"

"Yes. For a time, the wolves found solace here. They were not welcomed by the coven, so our witches stayed away. The wolves stayed in the sacred space, hiding from mankind, the druid's spell keeping others away, for a time," Elswyth explained.

"What happened?" I asked.

"Lady Charlotte grew tired of her game—and its unexpected complications—and sent the pack away."

"But there is a wolf on the moor. Has the pack returned?"

"No," Afwyn said. She looked at the others. I could see the worry and apprehension in her face.

"As we agreed," Cad, the green-robed elemental, told her.

"Very well," she said then motioned Aife. The goddess exited the stones, moving deep into the fog. As she went, I realized she wasn't really walking, she was floating.

Reverent.

Reverent.

A few moments later, the woman returned holding the hand of a boy who looked to be about seven years of age. He was a sweet thing, all arms and legs, a tangle of soft yellow hair on his head…and glowing red eyes.

"Agent Louvel, I'm pleased to introduce you to Jericho," Afwyn said.

I stared at the child—the werewolf child—who was fiddling nervously with the hem of his waistcoat. I sized the boy over from head to toe, from his pale blond hair to the six fingers on his right hand.

"He's…"

"Jericho's father was the alpha of the pack that passed through this place. And his mother—"

"Lady Charlotte?"

Afwyn inclined her head. "Yes, Lady Charlotte."

"But why is he out here?"

"She abandoned the baby to the pack. The pack abandoned the boy to us."

"Hell's bells." A hard knot tied in my stomach.

"Lady Charlotte's motivations are, no doubt, obvious. The child is an unwanted burden, a scandal. The pack's alpha—Lady Charlotte's lover—was killed by his beta. The new alpha did not want to raise the old leader's bastard child. The child is a lycan, Agent Louvel. Neither bitten nor born of pureblooded parents, he is neither human nor wolf. He was outcast as a wee thing by the pack. We intervened, made a case for the child's life. The pack left the child to us when they departed. Lady Charlotte pretends to know nothing of the boy. We have hidden him from everyone. But now he is coming of age, and we must make a choice. He must go with us to the Otherworld and stay there, or he must find his way in the world of wolves."

Astonished, I stared at the child. The werewolves I knew were of the bitten or pureblood variety. I had heard of lycans, wolves born of mixed parents, but had never met one. The boy was the first true lycan I had ever seen.

The child, who had been listening intently, suddenly said, "I'm not a lycan. I am a Cabell. I will make my mother see me," he said and then huffed a dark and wolfy sound. The noise was entirely endearing.

Afwyn sighed sadly. "We need your help, Clemeny Louvel."

"So I see," I said then turned to the boy. "You may want your mother to see you, but growling at and frightening your uncle, Lord Cabell, half to death won't help."

The boy puffed air through his lips and scowled at me.

"Not to mention, you could have been killed," I added, giving him a scolding look.

"The other lady missed."

"Yes, but you got lucky. She doesn't usually miss," I said then turned back to Afwyn. "What do want me to do? Charlotte Cabell is not going to accept this child."

"We know. You must take Jericho to the alpha in London. We understand the Templars rule this land now. He will be safe among the holy brotherhood. They will guide him, train him, give him a life where we cannot."

I looked at the boy. He looked so much like his uncle. "Lord Cabell doesn't know about Jericho?"

The elemental shook her head. "No. He was absent during Charlotte's pregnancy and for a long time afterward."

"I..." I looked at the child. A lycan. Half-wolf, half-human. All in all, he was just a little boy with a chip on his shoulder and a broken smile. He had been abandoned by his mother. It was only because of the benevolence of strangers that he was still alive. The child of a werewolf and woman, he was lost.

One day, maybe, Edison Cabell would see him. Maybe. But not yet.

"Jericho," I said, slipping my silver knife into my belt. I stepped toward the boy who braced himself, not for my movements, but for my words. I knelt. "I'm like you. I don't know my parents. I was left behind. A kind woman took me in, raised me. I understand what you're feeling. I can help you."

"Help me how?"

"Lady Afwyn spoke of the Templars. We can go to them. They are wolves, like you, but they're good. They will guide you, help you to control your gift."

The boy stared at me. A flash of red crossed his eyes. "Gift? This is no gift. My mother abandoned me because of what I am!"

His words rocked my soul. "Sometimes parents abandon their children because of what's missing inside them, not because of something missing inside you. I *can* help you, and I will if you will let me."

The boy looked back at the elementals. "I want Lady Charlotte to see me. I want to see my mother."

"She will not see you, Jericho," Cad told him.

"Are we certain?" I asked Afwyn. "Has anyone pressed Lady Charlotte on the matter?"

She nodded stoically, and for a moment, her eyes turned a dark, slate color. "I'm certain."

"But Agent Louvel can take you somewhere safe. We love you, but it is time," Odgaddeau told the boy.

Jericho crossed his arms and said nothing.

Afwyn wrapped her arms around him, kissed his head, then looked at me. "I have raised him since he was small. We have all watched out for him. But we are... This is not something we can do anymore. This is beyond us."

I looked at the child. "You must make me a promise."

The boy clenched his jaw.

"You must promise not to return to Cabell Manor. You could get hurt. You must not return there, not now. One day, perhaps, but not now."

"Fine," he said stiffly.

"I can meet you in the village tomorrow morning," Afwyn told me.

"Oh, Afwyn, are you sure?" Elswyth asked, worry

marring her face. As the sun had continued to sink below the horizon, the elementals had grown increasingly translucent. Blue, silver, gold, and green light surrounded them.

"It will tax me, but I will manage," Afwyn said.

I nodded to her. "I'll send a message to Templar Square, and tell them to expect us."

She inclined her head toward me. "Thank you. But now it's time to go, Agent," she told me, motioning that we should return to the ruins.

I looked at the others. "It has been an honor to meet you."

They inclined their heads to me.

"We will whisper to the spirits. You will find your way back to Cabell Manor unscathed," Cad told me.

"Thank you."

As we walked back toward the ruin, I noticed that even more blue lights had appeared. They spun in circles, zipping back and forth. The stones shimmered with magical light.

"An ancient place hidden in the modern world. We don't have long now. When the modern world comes, it will be the end of us. That is why the boy must leave. We aren't long for this world, Clemeny Louvel.

"I'm sorry to ask for your help with the child. I love him, but he has taken to roaming the fens, haunting the manor. With the curse, I am sure everyone is spooked.

When you and your partner arrived, I knew I must act. But then the wind whispered your name. It told me I could depend on you."

I stopped. "Why? Why did the wind whisper my name? Why can I be depended upon? That light inside me... What is it?"

"Are you ready to know?"

"Yes."

"Then follow your dreams. They'll lead you to answers."

The image of Glastonbury—and Lionheart—came back to me once more. "Thank you."

We walked through the ruin to the road on the other side. The trail disappeared down into the mist. Afwyn gestured before her. At once, the mists parted, allowing me a path through. "Meet me tomorrow morning at the airship tower."

"I will," I said, then headed back into the mist.

In the moonlight, it was easy to see the way. As I went, the path continued to clear before me. The elementals had been true to their word. The enchantment didn't touch me.

But as I walked, I caught soft whispers in the air.

Clemeny.

Clemeny, come home.

I closed my eyes. It was not the spell. It was the other voice that whispered to me. I didn't know what or whom was speaking to me. But at least now I knew what the voices wanted.

Clemeny.

"I tell you what, if you want me to come to the summer country and sort all this mess out, bring Lionheart home. Now," I said, turning to the mist around me, watching phantom-like shapes that twisted and twirled.

No answer.

I glared at the mist. "That's what I thought."

Feeling suddenly frustrated, I turned and stalked back toward the manor. With each step, I felt my frustration rise. How could Lady Charlotte just abandon her child like that? How could she play around with a werewolf—knowing he was a werewolf—then just expect everything to go well? Such creatures were not objects of curiosity. They were men with hearts and minds of their own. She had no business falling in love with a werewolf. She should have known it would never work, that she wouldn't be able to have a normal life with him, let alone a child. And then she just abandoned them both. Did she even know her father's child was dead? Didn't she pine for him with every breath, worry about him every minute, and wait and wonder where he was? Didn't she feel pain in her chest every time she thought she might not see him again? And her own child… Didn't she feel something? No. She was foolish and careless. A tourist. Apt title. And now here I was, trying to find a way to protect the boy she had abandoned. Me. I had been sucked into the mist to clean up her problem. I wouldn't stay at Cabell Manor a minute more than I had to. Tomorrow morning, I would take the lycan child to London. I'd send a message to Edwin. I didn't want to hurt him, but I couldn't tolerate being near that woman. I could never be around someone who disregarded the preternatural as toys. They weren't. They were people with minds, and hearts, and souls. They were people who deserved to be loved just like the rest of us. Just because they were different, it didn't make them bad or wrong.

I stopped.

My heart was beating so hard I could hear it in my ears.

I looked up at the moon.

No, there was nothing wrong with loving a preternatural.

Nothing wrong at all.

CHAPTER 20
In the Garden

I slipped across the misty fen, arriving at the manor once more. The silhouette of the building appeared on the horizon, backed by the almost full moon. The angel on the top of the house was bathed in moonbeams. Silver light broke through the mist, casting a bluish haze on the place. The windows of the house stared like empty eyes out onto the fen.

Light passed one of the upper windows as someone moved in and out of the room with a lantern.

When I reached the back gate, I slipped quietly inside, keeping in mind there was a pair of mechanical gargoyles prowling. Creepy devils, I'd rather avoid anything I couldn't take down with a silver bullet. Following the primly kept garden paths, I made my way past the reflection pools, weaving around the statues.

My senses, however, felt the presence of another in the garden with me.

I slowed to a stop then turned and looked, gazing around the foggy garden. In the distance, I heard the click of the mechanical gargoyles' gears and saw a flash of blue eyes in the mist. I stopped to watch the clockwork guardian prowl. How curious a creation. Yet still, there was something else there. I could feel something besides the machine.

If I spoke, it would trigger the gargoyle's alarm. Still, who in the world would be out here now? Had the boy gotten loose once more?

I eyed the place closely with my mooneye.

Witches. Elementals. Werewolves. Humans. Spirits. Could have been anyone out there. But at the moment, they weren't moving, weren't intervening. Best to leave well enough alone.

I pulled my silver blade, ignoring the tingling feeling on my back of my neck, and headed toward the house. Spotting the second gargoyle perched near the front door, I hesitated, unsure what to do. But a rustle in the garden not far from the gate caught the machine's attention, and it went off to investigate.

Taking my chance, I rushed to the door.

But now my curiosity was piqued. Rabbit or monster? What had the clockwork device heard? I scanned the mist, but there was nothing there. Nothing more than a heavy feeling that lingered on my senses.

Suppressing a sigh, I headed inside.

CHAPTER 21

Harper in the Small Library with a Plan

Hoping to avoid Lord Cabell and Lady Charlotte, I tiptoed down the hallway toward the small library. It was already very late. I expected everyone was in bed, except Harper. But as I approached the library, I heard voices.

Wonderful.

I took a deep breath then opened the door.

On the other side, I found Harper, Lady Charlotte, Lord Cabell…and Edwin.

My heart skipped a beat.

They stood over a map laid out on the desk. Edwin's hands were laced behind his back as he considered Harper's words, but his brow was crinkled with worry. Harper was talking in hurried tones. She was nervous.

"Something interesting?" I asked.

Harper stopped mid-sentence. "Clemeny," she said, exhaling deeply.

My eyes met Edwin's. The wrinkle on his forehead disappeared at once.

"We were getting rather anxious about you," Lord Cabell said, crossing the room to greet me. "Agent Harper and Sir Edwin were about to go out to look for you, despite mine and Charlotte's repeated pleas of caution."

So, Lord Cabell and Lady Charlotte wanted to leave me on the fen to die? That was nice of them. "That's the job, sir. But all is well."

"So glad to hear it, so very glad. Here, let me pour you a drink," Lord Cabell said then headed for the bottle sitting on a cart nearby. "Edwin? A drink?"

"Yes, I do believe I'll take one now," he said, his voice tinged with relief. He crossed the room to greet me. As he did so, I saw Lady Charlotte's eyes follow him. There was annoyance in her gaze, especially when she noticed the affectionate look on Edwin's face.

"I wasn't expecting you until tomorrow," I told him.

"I thought you might want an extra hand. And then I arrived to find you had been lost in the mist. I almost lost my composure. Must you always find trouble?"

"Yes, but I'm not bloody and bruised, for once."

"Well, that is a relief."

"The matter is nearly sorted. We should talk later."

Edwin gently touched my arm, giving it the softest of squeezes. "I'm glad you're all right. And very glad to see you," Edwin's eyes spoke volumes as he stared at me. But there was more. There was an expression on his face I hadn't seen there before, a kind of nervous excitement.

"Are you all right?" I whispered.

He laced his hands behind his back once more. He smiled softly at me. "Now, I'm perfect."

"Here you are, Edwin," Lord Cabell said, handing his old friend a drink. "And one for you, Agent. Please don't leave us with bated breath. You must tell us what you found out in the mist."

I took the drink, sipping while I concocted a lie, then nodded. "It was an apparition, an echo of things long forgotten. You know how it is, Romans and druids running amuck, leaving behind bad spirits. You must have kicked it up in your visit to the ruins."

"Do you mean a ghost? How extraordinary," Lady Charlotte said.

I didn't look at her for fear my utter disgust would give me away. "Well, the ruins are an ancient, sacred place. So, unless you want to upset the spirits of ancient druids further, risking the ire of the old gods, you should appeal to the Historical Commission to earmark the land as a historical site and leave it be."

Harper raised a confused eyebrow. "An apparition? But we saw corporeal evid—"

"We were mistaken," I said, cutting her short and shooting her a *let's talk later, stop asking questions* look.

"So it's not the curse—or the anything else... monstrous," Lady Charlotte said.

I swallowed my rage. "I suppose that depends on how you define monstrous. Your family was warned not to return to the ruins. Seems like advice that should have been heeded."

Lord Cabell took a drink. "Blimey. I don't know what to say." He looked pale. While he tried to hide it, his hand was shaking.

"We should just pull down those stones and be done with that place," Lady Charlotte said with an annoyed glare. "Nothing but trouble has ever come to the Cabells from those old stones."

"Pull down a ring of standing stones? You'll risk the wrath of all the Celtic gods," Edwin remarked stiffly.

"Very true," I said, giving Lady Charlotte a sharp look.

Lady Charlotte frowned and looked away.

"We must set that land aside—for good," Lord Cabell said. "There will be no more debate about it. It's an important historical place. I won't develop the land anywhere near there."

I cast a glance at Lady Charlotte. She was staring into the fireplace. Her brother also looked at her, an inquisitive expression on his face. "Charlotte? Don't be irritated."

"I'm not."

"What is it then? Your ball can proceed as planned," Lord Cabell said.

She forced herself to smile. "It's nothing. Good. Very good. Well, if the spirit is put to rest, then we can proceed. As long as Agent Louvel is sure."

She turned to me, her eyes fishing my face. Did she suspect I'd learned something? She had hidden the child, hidden her dalliance with the werewolf, hidden it all. But did she suspect I knew? Was howling on the fen the very thing that had landed her in trouble in the first place.

"There is nothing to concern you on the moor now," I told her, my voice hard and flat.

She stared at me as she turned over my words. Part of her was dying to question me more. The other prayed her secret hadn't been revealed. "Very good. Well done, Agent," she said then rose. "Sir Edwin, I'm afraid I've had a hectic day, and my eyes are drifting. I hate to leave you so soon after you've arrived, but I'm afraid I must."

Edwin nodded to her. "Of course. Please, don't hesitate."

"And now, for the first night in many weeks, we will

all sleep soundly," Lord Cabell reassured his sister with a loving smile.

"Yes, you're right," Lady Charlotte said. Pausing to kiss her brother on the cheek, she waved goodnight to the rest of us then left the room.

Of course. Sleep soundly while the child you abandoned suffers. Why would that keep anyone awake at night?

"I, on the other hand, need to go warn the downstairs staff that the ball is still on," Lord Cabell said, setting aside his drink. "Will you excuse me?"

Edwin nodded to him while I gave him a tired smile.

We stilled, waiting for him to leave the room. The moment the door closed, Edwin and Harper looked at me.

"All right, Clemeny. Now, out with it," Harper said.

I eyed the door. "Are we sure we're alone?"

Edwin looked around the room then nodded.

"Well, there was a werewolf on the moor. And tomorrow, I will escort him to London."

"Wait, what? Then why did you lie? And where is the wolf?" Harper asked.

"The wolf is under the watch of an elemental. I'll meet her tomorrow at the airship tower in the village to collect her charge."

"An elemental," Harper said with a gasp.

"She—and the others—were local spirts once

worshipped as gods. They are barely hanging on. They still exist, but in the most rudimentary of forms."

"I don't think we have any record of an agent encountering an elemental," Edwin said. "And certainly not a local god."

"But is this all safe? How can an elemental control a werewolf?" Harper asked.

"It's complicated."

"But Clemeny—" Harper began.

"The werewolf is a seven-year-old lycan who is the heir to Cabell Manor."

Edwin and Harper stared at me.

"Lord Cabell's...heir?" Harper asked.

"Yes and no. His heir, but not his son. The boy is Lady Charlotte's child."

Edwin coughed then coughed again. "How do you know?" he asked.

I relayed the tale the Afwyn had shared with me.

"Is she to be trusted?" Harper asked. "Is she telling the truth?"

"She has no reason to lie. And the boy looks like his mother—and uncle. I'll take the child to the Templars. They will know how to raise the boy."

"Even though he is a lycan?" Edwin asked.

"I trust the Templars to do the right thing."

"A human and a werewolf," Harper said.

"A lycan," I said then shrugged. I tried to look

nonchalant, but there was a heavy feeling in my stomach. "Lycans are not common but not unthinkable."

Harper shook her head. "But Lady Charlotte... I can't believe she just abandoned her child like that."

I nodded to her.

"I guess some things are more important than blood," I said.

Harper frowned. "I can't imagine what. Lycan or not, he's still just a boy."

"Lycan or human, a child born out of wedlock would have been a scandal for Lady Charlotte," Edwin said.

"Well, God forbid," Harper said, sounding exasperated.

I was glad she said it because I was certainly thinking it.

Edwin frowned, unsure what to say. After a moment, he turned to me. "I'm sorry to hear you need to leave. I had hoped you would stay on for the ball. I suppose the whole affair is tarnished now."

"I can take the boy to Temple Square," Harper offered. "Blackwood doesn't seem to completely despise me or ignore me like Lionheart used to. We'll go together and meet the elemental in the morning. I confess, I'm dying to see her, if you think she won't mind. I'll take the child, if they'll permit it."

A sudden panic gripped me. I really, really wanted

to leave. Part of me was praying Harper would stop talking. But the other part of me noticed how forlornly Edwin was staring at me. He really wanted me to stay. "Don't you want to stay for the ball?" I asked Harper.

"Um. No. I think it's best if I bow out now," she said, her eyes full of unspoken words. Had Lord Cabell said something? Was she trying to escape this place as desperately as I was?

I raised an eyebrow at her.

She gave me a telling look. "It's better this way, as long as the elemental will agree."

I looked back at Edwin who was trying to remain calm but was looking very eagerly at me all the same.

"I can't say I'm much inclined to be friendly toward Lady Charlotte now," I admitted, turning to Edwin.

"Were you ever?" Harper asked.

I winked at her over my shoulder.

"I understand, but there are some people coming I'd like you to meet. My…godmother is planning to attend. I just thought… If you stayed, I would be grateful," Edwin said nervously. "Edison is a good friend. Charlotte has always been problematic," he said then shook his hand. "I believe she once had her cap set at me, but I think she liked me more out of an interest in my occupation than for myself, honestly. Regardless, will you stay, Clemeny?"

Moved by his vulnerability, especially in front of

Harper, I turned to my partner. I raised an eyebrow at her.

"See us off in the morning," Harper said. "Let's make sure this elemental is okay with me taking over. If she is, then stay. Blackwood and I can handle this. The Templars need to get used to me."

I nodded. "All right."

"Well, with that settled, who wants another drink?" Edwin asked.

Harper gently gripped her stomach. "Definitely, not me."

CHAPTER 22
Farewell

That night, nothing prowled the fens beyond the gardens at Cabell Manor. It had been a long day. I was exhausted, emotional, and ready to be done with this case. But the look in Edwin's eyes had made me say yes. That same look unnerved me. I cared for Edwin, I really did. But something about that look scared me.

Leaving Edwin behind to catch up with Lord Edison, I headed to bed.

Harper and I woke just after sunrise and started getting ready. We were halfway dressed when Emma, the maid, appeared.

"Oh, Agents. I dare say, you keep such odd hours," she said, finding us both nearly ready to head out.

"I was just about to pop in and see if we could get a transport to the village," I told her.

"Of course. Let me ask the driver to come around," Emma said.

"Someone will need to take down Agent Harper's cases. She's returning to London," I added.

"It's no trouble. I can get them," Harper protested.

"No, Agent. We'll see to it. Lady Charlotte is still abed, but Lord Cabell is up early. Will you be leaving soon too, Agent Louvel?"

"No, I'll stay on for the ball."

"Ah, yes. The ball," she said, raising and lowering her eyebrows in amusement. "I did fuss with your gown a bit. It's all ready for you. But I didn't see your mask."

"Mask?" I asked.

Emma nodded. "It's a masked ball. Didn't you know?"

"No, I did not."

"How quaint," Harper commented under her breath as she fussed with her cases.

"Don't worry, Agent. I'll find something for you. Now, let me see about the carriage," Emma said then turned and headed back downstairs.

"You know," I said, turning to Harper, "you could probably drop the boy to the Templars then catch an agency transport back to the manor in time for the ball."

"I could, but I don't want to. Lord Cabell is a nice man but no. And Lady Charlotte disgusts me."

"You tell me."

Harper nodded. "So, Agent Hunter's godmother then?"

"So it seems."

"Are you ready?"

"Well, I suppose I had to meet his family at some point, but I—"

"No, no, are you ready?"

"For?"

"Don't be daft, Clem. You know where all this is headed."

"I…" Was she right? No, surely not yet. I couldn't even conceive of a proposal without knowing what had happened to Lionheart.

"Don't rush anything," Harper said. "You have a lot to think through."

"Yes."

"Just trust your instincts."

"Even if they have strange ideas?"

"Have your strange ideas ever failed you before?"

"Not that I can think of."

"Then I think you have your answer."

There was a knock on the door.

"Footman, Agents. I'm here for Agent Harper's bags," a boy called.

"I'm ready. Let's go," Harper told me. With that, we headed downstairs.

Just as we reached the main foyer, Lord Cabell appeared.

"Agent Harper. Frances just informed me that you're leaving. I'm so very sorry to hear it. Can't you stay for the ball?" he asked, looking genuinely disappointed. For a moment, I felt sorry for him. But just for a moment.

"I'm sorry. I'm needed in London. I'll be taking an airship back this morning."

He nodded. "I'm told you're headed into the village now. I'm sorry that Charlotte isn't here to see you off. I know she's so very grateful for your and Agent Louvel's work."

I wondered how she'd feel if she knew we were about to take custody of her son.

"Please send her my thanks for your hospitality," Harper said. "And thank you, Lord Cabell."

"It was my pleasure. You'll have to come to see us again under more hospitable circumstances."

Mister Frances appeared at the door, motioning to indicate that the driver was ready.

"Agent Louvel, Edwin tells me you'll be staying on. Very good. Lady Chadwick, his godmother, should be arriving soon. You'll adore her. All the guests will start floating in today in anticipation of the merriment."

I tried to conjure up an image of Lady Chadwick. All I could come up with was a cleaned up version of the

Dís, which didn't seem quite right. But the thought did make me smile.

"I'll be back soon," I said then motioned to Harper that we really needed to get the hell out of there.

Harper waved farewell to Lord Cabell then we headed outside to the carriage. Harper and I slipped into the back. Once we settled in and the driver took off, we sighed simultaneously, then laughed that we did so.

"I'm relishing my escape. But you…"

"I'm sighing in anticipation of Lady Chadwick staring at my eye like she was looking at a cyclops."

Harper laughed loudly. "Sorry, but that was funny. You'll be fine."

"Well, it is a masked ball, so at least I'll have that going for me."

"Clemeny," Harper said, shaking her head.

The carriage moved quickly across the fenlands toward the nearby town. I glanced out at the endless stretch of wetlands covered in mist. The leaves on what few trees there were had changed color from dull orange to listless brown.

I sighed, feeling jealous of Harper's escape.

The carriage arrived at the village a short while later. Harper instructed the driver to take us to the airship tower. When we arrived, I spotted an aging airship tethered overhead. Sitting on a bench at the base of the tower was Afwyn the elemental, and the lycan boy, both of whom were eating ice cream cones.

"Well, that's something you don't see every day," Harper whispered.

"I'm just jealous they didn't buy one for me."

"It's eight o'clock in the morning. Are you sure about the boy? He looks like a cherub not a lycan."

"Just wait until moonrise."

Harper took her bags from the driver, and we cautiously approached the pair. The boy, who was concentrating on his ice cream, barely gave us a passing glance. Afwyn rose, dropped what was left of the treat into the trash receptacle nearby—to my great sadness—and moved to greet us. "Agent Louvel," she said, nodding to me. "And "Agent Harper?"

Harper nodded.

"I'm Afwyn."

"My Lady," Harper said, inclining her head to the elemental.

"I hope it won't be a problem, Afwyn, but Agent Harper will journey with Jericho to London. I need to stay on at the manor a bit longer," I said. "I'll rejoin them in the city in a couple of days."

Afwyn eyed Harper closely.

"Agent Harper is more than capable."

Afwyn turned, tilting her head as if she were listening to something, then nodded. "Very well. But you'll check on the boy, Agent Louvel? I have your word?"

"Yes. You have my promise. I will keep an eye on him. Always."

Harper looked at me out of the corner of her eye.

"Very well," Afwyn said then turned to Jericho. "This is Agent Harper," she told the boy, motioning to Harper. "She will take you to London. Agent Louvel will come to see you in a few days."

The boy eyed Harper then me. "Fine," he said then went back to eating.

"It's time to go now," Afwyn told him.

"I want to finish my ice cream," he replied.

"I'm sorry. It's time to go. The captain is waiting, and you can't take the ice cream on the airship," she said then reached out for what was left of the ice cream cone.

To my surprise, he paused mid-lick and let out a low growl. For a moment, his eyes flashed red.

"Jericho," Afwyn whispered. "Manners."

"Ah," Harper muttered. "There it is."

"Told you," I whispered.

"Jericho, is that your name?" Harper said, approaching the child who looked suspiciously at her out of the corner of his eye. "I'm Elaine. I'll be flying with you to London. Do you like toffee? I have toffee in my bag. Surely the captain won't mind a bit of candy.

Shall we go up and have a look at the airship? They're fun to ride on. Ever been on one before?"

The boy paused mid-lick and studied Harper. "How much toffee do you have?"

Harper smiled. "A whole bag."

"Never offered me any," I complained lightly.

"Well, aren't you glad I have them now?" she shot back, giving me a look, then turned her attention back to the boy. "Shall we go up and have some?"

"Can I have the whole bag?"

An alpha in the making.

"Of course. But first, I think you must make your goodbyes."

Reluctantly, the boy rose and tossed his ice cream in the trash. He then turned and looked at Afwyn. "I'll see you soon, right?"

"Maybe not so soon, but you will see me again."

The boy wrapped his arms around her waist and hugged her tight. "Love you," he whispered.

"I love you too," Afwyn replied. I heard her choke back her heartbreak.

Jericho let go of Afwyn and turned to Harper. "Can I have a piece of toffee now?"

"Once we get on the airship, I'll give you the bag."

"All right," the boy said then headed toward the platform. He paused and looked back at Afwyn. His eyes lingered on her for a long moment. He waved to her then headed to the platform.

"Be safe," I called to Harper.

She waved to me then followed behind the lycan.

A few moments later, the lift rose, taking Harper and Jericho to the airship.

I turned and looked at Afwyn. "Are you all right?"

She nodded, but my mooneye could see she was fading. It appeared as if she was phasing in and out. She held on tight to her hooked staff.

"I'll keep my word," I whispered.

Afwyn set her hand on my arm. "I know," she said. She gave me a squeeze then, moving slowly, she turned and walked away from me. Her path took her in the direction of the sunrise. I winced as I watched her go. For a few moments, I could see her clearly, but then she seemed to dissolve into the sunlight and was gone.

Sighing, I headed back to the carriage. The driver, who'd been reading a novel, set the book down when I returned.

"Back to the manor, Agent?" he asked.

"Yes. But I need to pick up something first," I said, grinning as I pulled out my coin purse. "Care for ice cream?"

CHAPTER 23
Odd is as Odd Does

The carriage driver and I rode back to Cabell Manor eating ice cream, chatting about the weather, and gossiping about how much all the servants at Cabell Manor disliked Lady Charlotte's All Hallows Ball. Apparently, given the family curse, most of the servants thought her playing around with the occult would bring them all bad luck.

"Haunted place, anyway," the driver said. "I've only been here a year. Aside from Mister Frances, Missus Carroll, and a couple of the maids, most of the staff has been here less time than me."

"Is that right?"

"Lady Charlotte is very odd and difficult to please, and Lord Cabell—who seems like a decent enough chap—is never here. I heard his Lordship say he's planning to go to India. I've started to look around for a new position myself."

"Not keen to go to India with him?"

The man laughed. "No, Agent. I'm not. But until I find something... Well, I'm glad you and your partner came. We were all a bit nervous at first, but Mister Aaron said you and Miss Harper were nice ladies. And it was quiet on the fen last night."

"So it was. And so it should remain."

"As long as Lady Charlotte doesn't conjure some devil into our midst. You know, she employs a fortuneteller to come for the ball. She told all the servants we could visit the woman if we wanted. Like hell I will."

"Don't you believe in the occult, Mister Wallace?" I asked the driver.

"I do. Which is why I don't like any of this. The rich have odd tastes."

He had no idea.

"Just because someone is odd, it doesn't necessarily make them bad," I said, reassuring the man. Of course, in Lady Charlotte's case, he was absolutely right.

"That's true. It just makes them crave ice cream for breakfast," the driver said with a laugh.

"Hey, you're eating too!"

"I couldn't resist. They had pistachio, and you were buying."

"Nothing odd about saying yes to free ice cream," I said with a good-natured chuckle, which he joined.

"Speaking of odd," Mister Wallace said as we drove up the drive toward the manor. Carriages, servants, horses, and even a few steam cars packed the front of the house. "Oh, joy. Lady Chadwick is here."

"Where?"

"Inside, I reckon. That's her driver."

"Don't you like her?"

"Ever met her?"

I shook my head.

"Well," he said, eyeing me over. "You'll see for yourself. Nothing pleases that woman. You might want to —" He pointed to my cheek. "You've got a bit of chocolate there."

"Approached the ice cream with too much passion, I guess."

He chuckled.

I wiped the back of my hand across my cheek. "Why don't you take the carriage around back. I'll go up the servant's stairwell."

"Are you sure?"

"I am totally, completely sure," I said, eyeing the well-dressed lords and ladies milling about in front of the house.

Hell's bells. I should have gone back to London with Harper.

I sneaked up the back stairwell to my room to find that Emma had laid out my green dress. Quickly shimmying out of my clothes, I pulled the gown on only to realize the hem had been repaired and, by some miracle, the burn stain on the arm was far less noticeable. When I saw Emma again, I'd have to thank her.

Struggling with the laces, I had nearly finished dressing when there was a knock on the door.

Pulling myself together, I went to the door to find Edwin there.

"Here you are. I was confused when they sent me to this part of the house looking for you. Is this where Lady Charlotte roomed you and Harper?" he asked, frowning at the small space with its double beds.

"Cozy, isn't it?"

Edwin frowned. "I'm sorry, Clemeny. I should have come out with you from the start. Victoria is having some trouble in the far reaches of the empire. I was scheduled to attend a meeting and couldn't miss it."

"What kind of trouble?"

"Well, I'm not quite sure yet. We're assembling a team to investigate."

"Where?"

"India."

"Isn't Lord Cabell also headed to India?"

"So he is. I was going to ask Harper if she wanted to go."

I laughed. "Good luck."

Edwin chuckled. "You're right," he said then eyed the room once more. "I should have the maids move you."

"It's nothing. And it's just for one more night."

Edwin sighed. "They're meeting in the parlor before luncheon. Will you come down?"

I smoothed down the front of my dress, suddenly feeling incredibly awkward. I could handle a nest of vampires, a pack pit fight, or even some Viking werewolves, but parlor pleasantries?

Edwin eyed me over. "The back of your dress… Your top lace appears undone. Didn't you have a lady's maid to help?"

I laughed. "There was a girl, but I'm sure she's busy with the *real* ladies."

"Please, allow me," Edwin said, turning me gently around.

Moving carefully, Edwin redid the laces on my back.

"You'll tell me if it's too tight. I confess, I can't tell where you begin and the gown ends."

I chuckled. "As long as I can still breathe, all will be well."

"I'm sorry to ask you to endure this. My godmother is all the family I have left here now. I want you to meet, but she is rather traditional. I have told her about you, but that doesn't mean she'll be…"

Kind. Accepting. Polite. "I understand."

"Thank you for your patience."

I smiled. Edwin meant the world to me. I wanted him to be happy, but part of me wondered if I was doing the right thing. Was it right for me to meet his family? After all, it wasn't as if we were engaged. We were just…close. I cared for Edwin, I really did, I just wasn't sure where any of this was heading.

Or where I even wanted it to go.

Things had felt clear before.

Now…

I closed my eyes. Once more, an image of Lionheart passed through my mind. Dammit, nothing was clear anymore.

"I think you're all in, m'lady," Edwin said with a laugh.

"Thank you," I replied. I exhaled deeply then turned to face Edwin who was smiling sweetly at me, the expression evoking his dimples.

Moving carefully, he reached out and touched my chin.

"What?" I whispered.

"Just… I liked helping you with your dress."

My stomach tied into a knot. "I liked your help."

Edwin offered his arm to me. "Shall we?"

"May the gods help me," I said, my mind going to the five gods—literally—I had met on the moor. Well, they were as good as any.

Afwyn, help me through this day.

Outside my window, a loon called.

CHAPTER 24
Clemeny in the Parlor with Lady Chadwick

We entered the busy room to find it swimming with posh lords and ladies. Edwin caught Lord Cabell's eye. Lord Cabell lifted his drink to welcome us then turned to the group of men surrounding him, laughing and talking all the while.

Edison Cabell was a good man. One day in the future, I think Edison Cabell could meet his nephew. Maybe.

Lady Charlotte, on the other hand, was sitting on the opposite side of the room, a group of well-dressed ladies surrounding her. She was speaking in a low tone. She paused, and the cluster of women looked over their shoulders at me.

Something inside me hardened, and I had to fight off the urge to out Lady Charlotte's secret then and there.

But the other part of me, Felice Louvel's granddaughter, felt embarrassed. Stupid, really. I didn't care about this kind of thing. I had more important issues to take care of than worrying about my hair or the latest fashion, but still. The delicate, younger version of me got rosy-cheeked when all the fancy ladies looked down their noses at me. The truth was, in that room, I felt small.

"Is it too early to drink?" I whispered to Edwin.

"It isn't the custom for ladies to imbibe at this time. At lunch, there will be wine. I say, Clem, are you all right? Your face is red. Did I pull the laces too tight?"

"No. I'm fine."

"Ah, there she is," Edwin said, motioning with his chin to the other corner of the room. "Shall we?"

"Of course."

I should have gone to London with Harper.

Edwin and I crossed the room to join an aged matriarch who was bedecked in heaps of silk and jewels, her hands resting on a cane. She looked up at Lord Samson with bored exasperation written all over her face.

Well, at least we had one thing in common.

Catching sight of Edwin out of the corner of her eye, the grey-haired woman rose, steadied herself with her walking stick, and pushed around Lord Samson without another word. The Lord, who looked a bit confused at being dismissed so out of hand—no doubt he'd been so lost in his pontifications that he hadn't realized he didn't really have an audience—tottered off to find another mark.

"Edwin," the woman said warmly, approaching him with her arm extended.

Edwin went to her, kissing the woman on her soft, wrinkled cheek. "Godmother, I am so pleased to see you doing well."

"Well? Well? Well enough, I suppose. But I am here all the same, and glad to see you. My goodness, how much you look like your late grandfather with each passing year. You know, had it not been for the vulture, your grandmother, we would have married."

"Yes, Lady Chadwick, you have told me many times."

"Oh, dear Edwin, just look at you. You must come to see me more often. You work too much—like a commoner, my dear—it's obscene."

"I work for Her Majesty. Is that not noble?"

"Oh, well, I suppose. Now, where is this woman you told me—" she began then looked around Edwin at me. For a moment, her brow flexed as she took me in from head to toe, her eyes lingering on my gown then on my face. She frowned heavily, shook her head, then looked behind me. She was looking for someone more suitable. *I* couldn't possibly be the girl.

"Godmother, may I introduce Miss Clemeny Louvel?" Edwin said, gently reaching for me.

My heart thudding in my chest, I stepped forward.

Lady Chadwick froze, the expression on her face showing that she could not believe what she was hearing, then looked back at me. "Oh," she said.

I swallowed hard then curtsied—awkwardly. "Lady Chadwick," I said.

"Oh. Yes. Oh my. So, this is your…friend?"

"Yes. Miss Louvel works at the Agency."

"A subordinate?"

"Well," Edwin said then shifted uncomfortably, lacing his hands behind his back. "Miss Louvel is in line to be promoted to my level. She is the head of her division."

"Of her division. And what is it you do, my dear?" she asked, looking at me.

"Law enforcement."

"Oh. Oh my. Just like Edwin."

"For the crown, Godmother. Like me, Miss Louvel works at the behest of Her Majesty."

"Yes. Well. I suppose one must make money somehow," she said then eyed my dress. "Pity when it's not spent where it should be," she added under her breath. "And what does your family do, Miss Louvel?"

"It's only my grandmother and me, My Lady. My grandmother is active with our church."

"Louvel. That's an unusual name."

"It's French," I replied.

Lady Chadwick recoiled. "French. You're French?"

"Not exactly. My grandmother is French."

"That makes you French, my dear."

"My grandmother and I are not related. I am adopted."

"From where?"

"The doorstep of a church."

"Edwin, help me back to my seat," Lady Chadwick said then, reaching out for him.

Good lord, I'd knocked the woman off her feet.

"Shall I get you some water?" I asked.

"Yes, yes," the woman called lightly, shooing me away with a wave of her hand.

I went to the sideboard where I found Niles serving.

"Water, please," I told him.

"How is it going with the dowager?" he asked as he poured me a glass.

"Not well. I just nearly made her faint."

He chuckled then motioned to a panel at the side of the room. "Servant's stairwell. Down and to the left if you need something more than water to get through."

"Can't you just slip me a flask?"

He chuckled. "Chin up, Agent. Didn't you just thrash some monster out on the fen?"

"So to speak," I said then took the drink from his hand. "Thanks," I added then headed back across the room.

Edwin was sitting in the chair beside Lady Chadwick who appeared to be haranguing him in a whisper.

"Completely unsuitable. Absolutely not. It cannot happen," Lady Chadwick was telling him in a low, but earnest tone, when I returned.

I hesitated.

No need to guess what that was about.

Edwin turned to me. He looked pale and shaken, but he smiled nonetheless.

"Here you are, Lady Chadwick," I said, handing her the glass. To my surprise, my hand was trembling. Inhaling, I steadied it.

"Thank you, Miss Louvel," she said, taking the cup. She sipped but gave Edwin a hard look at the same time.

"I'm terribly sorry. I've forgotten something I need to attend to. Lady Chadwick, if you'll please forgive me, I need to attend to a matter at once. I'll see you both at luncheon," I said then moved to go.

Edwin rose. "Clemeny?"

"Let her go," Lady Chadwick hissed under her breath.

"It's nothing. I just need to take note of something for the case before I forget. I'll see you soon," I said, then turned and left the room.

As I went, I felt Lady Charlotte's eyes on me. I didn't

have to look at her to see her smug smile. I could feel her gaze burning a hole in my back.

I exited the parlor then headed toward the small library. Halfway there, I paused.

I turned and went to the back of the house. Pushing open the doors, I exited onto the veranda. At once, I could breathe. The air was thick with mist. Even though it was daytime, the fog snaked around the angels and statues like it was alive. Setting my hand on my stomach, I breathed in and out.

Coward. I was a coward. I had let that old woman have the better of me in an instant.

Exhaling deeply, I stepped down into the garden until I found a bench in front of one of the reflecting pools. The water was still and grey. There was nothing to reflect here, no light, no color, just the grey hue of this place.

I really, really should have gone back with Harper.

Closing my eyes, I listened to the soft calls of the marsh birds and the song of the croaking frogs. It was so still, so peaceful and authentic compared to the artifice inside the house.

I stayed outside for a long time. The gong for lunch came and went. When I finally felt confident everyone had adjourned for luncheon, I sneaked back inside and headed up the servant's stairwell back to my room.

Slipping inside, I found my red dress draped over

the end of my bed. On the bed sat a mask, a note lying beside it. I picked up the paper. The note was from the Emma, the maid. She'd found a mask for the ball for me. I lifted the mask and studied it. It was made of red satin and trimmed with black lace. There were black rosettes at the temples. It was perfect, except for the fact that my mooneye was going to shimmer like a gaudy bauble in the midst of all the perfect opulence, reminding everyone—including Lady Chadwick—of just how unsuitable I was.

I sat down on the bed and pulled out my knife. I cut long slashes along the left side over the left eye, mimicking the scar on my face. When I was done, I held out the mask and looked.

Now, it was perfect.

Now, it was me. Flawed. Common. Not good enough for the likes of Edwin.

I'd felt more at home among the elementals on the fen.

How ironic.

What was it Afwyn had said to me? That it was the light inside me that had shielded me from the druids' spells. Maybe my comfort around the preternaturals wasn't just a figment of my imagination. There was something different about me. And it truly was time for me to find out what.

I just didn't want to face it alone.

My dream came to mind once more. I remembered how vivid the image of Lionheart and me at Glastonbury had been, the feel of his hand in mine, and despite the fact that his eyes had flickered ruby red, I'd felt comforted by his presence. In the dream, I'd been scared. Until Lionheart had taken my hand.

I closed my eyes. To my great frustration, tears burned the corners.

I didn't belong here.

I didn't fit here.

Dammit. I didn't want to be here. What was I going to do now? Lionheart hadn't given me any choice. He'd just up and left. After all that, he'd left me behind.

I squeezed my eyes shut.

Richard, come back.

A knock on the door startled me.

"Agent Louvel?" a voice called.

It was Emma.

I quickly dashed the tears away. "Come in."

"Here you are. I checked for you in the small library, but it looked like all your things had been collected. Sir Edwin asked Niles to check on you, but the footmen are very busy. I think you've missed the lunch. Are you unwell?"

"No. I was just busy. I had to... I went back on the fen for a bit," I lied.

"Oh, I see. Can I bring you a tray?"

"No, thank you."

"I see you found the mask. It was among some old things downstairs. I thought it matched your dress—oh," she said, seeing the cuts I had made on the item.

"I needed it to match," I said, motioning to my eye.

She chuckled. "Shall I come back later and help you with your gown? I think they'll begin at seven."

I paused. Should I bother? Edwin hadn't even checked on me. He'd sent a servant. What the hell did that mean?

"I'm not sure."

"I'll come back. Just have a rest. I'll see that Sir Edwin is informed you're still busy with your work," she said then left.

I went to the window and looked outside.

"Clemeny Louvel, why are you still here?" I whispered to myself.

Edwin.

I was here for Edwin.

Where was he?

CHAPTER 25
Red as Roses

Emma returned—no sign of Edwin—later that day to help me dress for the ball.

I had packed and unpacked my bag about six times in the interim, feeling stupid and silly. After the sixth time, I decided to clean my guns while I decided whether to go to the ball or not.

And wait for Edwin.

Who never came.

I had about made up my mind to leave—I had cleaned all my weapons and sharpened my blade—when the time to decide finally came.

Emma eyed the weapons lying on the spare bed, gave a little shake of the head, then turned to the red dress which I'd hung on the wardrobe door. "Pretty frock. Dare say, it must have set you back a pretty penny."

"It was a gift."

"Oh, well, you must have a very generous family. Or a gift from a friend, perhaps?"

A werewolf.

"Friend."

"Shall we get you dressed?"

I stared at the dress. Why had I brought it? It wasn't for Edwin. That dress didn't belong here, and neither did I.

That dress was for someone else.

Sensing my hesitation, Emma said, "Don't let them intimidate you, Agent Louvel. Just look at all this," she said, motioning to the weapons I had laid out on the bed. "People like that don't live in the real world. We do. Don't allow them to make you feel less. Let's get you into that dress and give them something to see."

She was right.

Maybe.

"All right," I acquiesced.

"Good. We're all rooting for you downstairs," she said with a grin. "Oh!" she exclaimed then dipped her hand into her pocket, pulling out a flask. "Niles sent this," she said, handing it to me.

I uncorked it and took a sniff. "Mead?"

Emma nodded. "Liquid luck, he called it," she said then laughed. The maid set her hands on her hips and looked at me. "Now, sit down, and let me at that hair."

Lifting the flask, I took a swig of the strong spirits, then another, then sat.

One way or the other, tonight I was going to learn who Sir Edwin Hunter really was.

For good or for bad.

Music emanated from the ballroom as I made my way down the steps toward the grand entryway. Below, the elegant lords and ladies in their fine gowns and suits, with a startling variety of masks, swirled in a torrent of silk, diamonds, and lace. I felt for a moment like I was at a carnival. If it wasn't for all the candles, corn stalks, jack-o-lanterns, carved gourds, wheat shafts, bunches of colorful fall leaves, and other signs of autumn, that could have easily been true. My first masked ball. Somewhere, Grand-mère was beaming with pride.

As for me, I felt anything but pride. After all, I was no one—as Lady Chadwick seemed so pleased to remind me. I was an orphaned child turned werewolf-hunting brute. What was I doing in a room full of people who had Sir, Lord, or Lady before their names? Maybe I should tell *them* to call *me* Little Red.

I glanced around the room for Edwin. It was dreadfully hot for an autumn night. I tried to take a breath. Emma had a deft hand at dressing a lady. I looked beautiful, but I could barely breathe. Or maybe I was just nervous. Edwin hadn't come upstairs. Perhaps he didn't want me here anymore. I didn't care for the Cabells, or Lady Chadwick, or any of the rest of it, but I did care for Edwin. I had failed him in my first meeting with Lady Chadwick. I didn't want to embarrass him again.

Maybe it would just be better if I left.

Honestly, I wasn't sure what to do.

But I did know one thing. The red dress Lionheart had purchased for me was beautiful. If I was ever going to impress anyone, it would be tonight. More than the dress being stunning, wearing it made me feel beautiful. Lord knows, Lady Chadwick had rendered me the opposite in a single glance. But the dress made things right again.

My hand, covered in a long red satin glove, drifted up to my perfectly curled and bunched hair. Aside from my mooneye, I looked the part.

I was still scanning the room for Edwin when my mooneye spotted something in my periphery. A shadow passed out of the corner of my eye. At once, the palms of my hand started to tingle.

Wonderful.

I was going to have to slay something. It was bad enough Phillip Phillips had to ruin my blue dress. If some preternatural marred *this* gown, there would be hell to pay.

A figure wearing an elegant tuxedo and sporting a plague doctor's mask and hat moved through the crowd toward me. I didn't need to see his face to know it was Edwin. I had engraved the man's posture in my memory. But tonight, I could see in his movements that *Sir* Edwin was on display. And I wasn't yet sure how I felt about *Sir* Edwin.

Edwin stopped at the bottom of the stairs and looked at me.

"I… Clemeny, you look beautiful," he said. "I wasn't sure if you were going to come."

"I wasn't sure if I should come."

The mask, which only covered the top portion of his face, didn't hide Edwin's frown. "I'm sorry for earlier," he said then walked up the steps to me. "I was stunned by Lady Chadwick's rudeness. To be honest, I didn't know what to do."

"To be honest, I expected more backbone out of you," I said, shocked by my own words as they tumbled from my lips.

All day, I had been stewing in my emotions. Things with Edwin had been progressing, and I had been considering what I might say if Edwin proposed—even with the added complication of Richard just disappearing on me. But Edwin had stood by while Lady Chadwick sneered at me. And he had stayed with her throughout the day, leaving me forgotten. I was beginning to question his nature. Had I mistaken Edwin Hunter, demon slayer? Was he really Sir Edwin Hunter, baronet? Now I wasn't so sure. One man I loved. The other? Not a fan.

"That's fair," Edwin said. "I expected more out of myself. I hope you can forgive me. I can't tell you how pleased I am you've come down. You look so very beautiful."

"Looking rather dapper yourself," I said.

At that, Edwin smiled, a tremor of nervousness playing on his lips. He extended his hand once more. "Will you come in?"

"Yes. But I hope we don't have to mar our perfect attire," I said, scanning the room once more for whatever was lurking.

Edwin paused. "What do you mean? What is it?"

"I thought I saw... Well, I don't know what I saw. But there is something afoot."

"I'm not surprised. Half the aristocracy—and mostly unbeknownst even to them—carries faerie blood."

I stared at Edwin. "Is that true?"

He nodded. "The preternaturals are always drawn to the sophisticated set. Just ask Agent Rose. But we must also keep in mind that it is Samhain."

"Agent Rose? It could have easily been a spirit. I didn't see anyone, per se. Just a flash and a feeling."

"Your flashes and feelings are better than most people's facts," Edwin said.

"And what about you? Any hunches tonight?"

"I confess, having Lady Chadwick here has me all off kilter. I don't think I've ever been less certain of my hunches before."

"Well, then I'll do my best to guide you."

"Please. I'm quite lost without you, Clemeny Louvel," Edwin said with a nervous laugh, and the two of us headed toward the ballroom.

I exhaled deeply, feeling myself fall into an easy familiarity with Edwin once more. I was making too much of all this. Edwin hardly ever bothered with this life. This world was wholly disconnected from our day-to-day work. Hell, Edwin had even leant his massive estate, Willowbrook Park, to the Pellinore Division of the Red Capes. Edwin lived in my world now. Whether Lady Chadwick approved of me or not hardly mattered. Not really. What mattered was how I felt about Edwin and him about me. And I really, truly cared for him.

But even as I reminded myself of my affection for Edwin, another emotion tugged on my heart.

He's gone.

He left.

Forget him.

Remember what Quinn said. Werewolf hunters don't fall in love with werewolves.

"Ready?" Edwin asked as we neared the double doors.

I nodded.

With a flourish, the footmen bowed and opened the doors.

"Welcome to the All Hallows Ball," Edwin whispered.

CHAPTER 26
The All Hallows Ball

While I had seen the room in preparation, nothing prepared me for the cacophony of music, the kaleidoscope of light and colors, and the pure grandeur of the All Hallows Ball. If I hadn't begun to secretly—*okay, maybe not so secretly*—detest Lady Charlotte, I would have been impressed. In one corner, the musician, dressed as skeletal players, played a waltz, filling the room with delightful music. Every corner of the room was decorated festively. Like the entryway, bales of hay, wheat shafts, gourds and pumpkins, scarecrows, broomsticks, and more decorated the place. Pointed black witches' caps hung from the ceiling alongside shadowy crepe material posing as ghosts. The servants were in costume as well, angels and devils circling the ballroom carrying trays with flutes of champagne. One section of the ballroom had been cornered off for two women who were offering occultist services: tarot and palm reading. The entire scene was lavish but jarring.

"I suspect Lord Byron would have approved," Edwin said, referring to the late poet who'd been well-known for his wild parties and coursing ways.

"Didn't you tell me you attend every year?"

Edwin grinned. "It's fun to make light of the monstrous from time to time."

"Is it?" I wasn't so sure. "Care to have your palm read?" I asked, motioning to the fortunetellers.

Once more, that strange feeling nagged at me. I glanced around the room for any sign of…well, anything. There was something here. With everyone wearing masks, it was impossible to spot anything out of the ordinary in the crowd. The room was a sea of mermaids, jesters, peacocks, princesses, armored knights, goddesses, and more. Everyone was dressed in costume. Everyone looked monstrous. That was the point.

"Tonight, of all nights, I feel my fate is in my own hands," Edwin said, but then caught my distracted gaze. "Clemeny?"

"Do you feel…" I said then scanned around again. Maybe it was as Edwin said, that I could sense the faerie blood. But I wasn't sure. Whatever was in the room, I had felt a presence like this before. There was a true preternatural in our midst.

Catching my meaning, Edwin also glanced around the room. "No, I don't sense anything."

"Edwin," a gravelly female voice called from behind us.

I recognized it at once.

Lady Chadwick.

I took a deep breath then turned around.

Lady Chadwick approached us, her cane tapping on the floor as she went. Part of me suspected she'd just as soon beat me over the head with it as opposed to making small talk. She wore a glittering blue gown and a small, sparkling tiara.

"Godmother," he said, inclining his head to her.

"Edwin, I barely knew you," she scolded him.

"That is the general idea, Godmother."

She rolled her eyes. "A plague doctor? Really, Edwin, how morbid."

Edwin chuckled. "Morbid? You have had a look around?"

"Yes, yes," she said with a wave of the hand. "Playing at monsters. Have you guessed my costume?"

"I'm afraid not," Edwin replied.

Lady Chadwick turned to reveal a dainty set of wings on her back. "I'm the fairy godmother, of course."

Edwin chuckled lightly. "Does that make me a

cinder lad?" Edwin asked then turned to me. "What do you say to that, Miss Louvel?"

"Well, I—"

"Have you seen Lady Charlotte tonight? How lovely she looks," Lady Chadwick interrupted.

I swallowed my impulse to stab her.

Edwin stiffened. "No, I hadn't noticed her."

"There, you see," Lady Chadwick said, pointing to Lady Charlotte who was dressed like some kind of princess.

"Is she holding a kitten?" I asked, startled to see that Lady Charlotte's costume had been accessorized with a tiny black kitten who looked like it would rather be anywhere other than in her arms. "Poor creature."

Lady Chadwick scoffed. "I thought it was delightful," she said then turned her attention to me, looking down her nose as best she could. She eyed me up and down. "Miss Louvel. I see you're feeling better. And what are you dressed as?"

"A rose maiden."

"A rose in autumn. Well, that's…different. I see the mask fits though."

Lady, I could easily murder you in five seconds. I'm wearing two pistols, a knife, silver knuckledusters, and have a dagger between my breasts.

"A rose by any other name," Edwin said, lifting my gloved hand and laying a kiss thereon.

In an instant, my murderous intentions vanished.

Lady Chadwick frowned.

A moment later, the musicians switched the melody and called for the next song.

"Oh, Edwin, be sure to dance with Lady Charlotte as you always do. We wouldn't want to break with tradition."

Edwin stiffened. "Of course. But my first dance is with Miss Louvel, if she will have me," he said then extended his arm.

I smiled at him, giving Lady Chadwick a *go jump of a bridge* look, then joined Edwin on the dance floor.

"It's a group dance," Edwin said as we joined the others. "Are you familiar?"

Are you, Clemeny Louvel, lowbred and all, familiar with finer forms? "Of course. Felice Louvel would be appalled if I weren't."

"Sorry. Naturally. I just wanted to make sure you were comfortable," Edwin said, an apologetic look in his eye.

Wonderful.

I took my spot across from Edwin. I scanned up and down the line at all the fine lords and ladies. Lord Edison and Lady Charlotte, who was without her kitten accessory—luckily for the kitten—were also in the line.

Now, Grand-mère, let's see if we've got this right. God forbid I take a wrong step.

The musicians struck a cord, and the music began to play. Edwin and I stepped toward one another, setting our hands on each other's, and turned in a circle.

"I hope you know I'm so sorry about Lady Chadwick," Edwin whispered.

We twirled, Edwin and I leaving one another momentarily as we twisted around another set of partners. I found myself face to face with a young man wearing a rabbit mask.

"Good evening," the gentleman said politely, his bright blue eyes flashing from behind the rabbit mask.

"And to you," I said, suddenly feeling ill at ease with the masked ball. Maybe I'd seen one too many dark things to think it was a good idea. Scanning down the line, I saw King Arthur, a horse, an owl, a fairy tale prince, lots of princesses, and a frog. Everyone delighted in hiding himself or herself, pretending to be different, pretending to be something more.

Wasn't that what I was doing too, pretending to be something I wasn't?

What was I doing here with all these posh people? I belonged on the rooftops of London hunting bad people doing bad things. I wasn't meant for society life. If anything, I would be more comfortable chatting up the fortunetellers or having a drink with the servants.

But still.

There was Edwin.

We switched partners once more. Edwin and I were partnered again.

"Don't worry about Lady Chadwick," I told him.

"I just want to make sure you're at ease. I don't live in this world very often, but it is part of me."

I swallowed hard. "Of course."

"I just want you to be happy. I want to make sure you're comfortable with all of it."

I wasn't. But more than that, the look on Edwin's face, even half hidden by his mask, told me he was anxious.

I wasn't sure how to reply.

"Clemeny?" Edwin whispered.

The song shifted, calling for the partners to switch once more.

"We'll talk more later," Edwin said then turned to face his new partner, taking the arm of a woman who was dressed like Cleopatra.

I turned to find myself on the arm of a man dressed as a monk. The man nodded to me, then we wove down the line, switching partners again and again. In an effort to make Grand-mère proud, I kept my footing and moved with the flow of the dance. But at the same time, my skin began to prickle. The palms of my hands and bottoms of my feet felt like they were on fire. There was something here. Trying to keep pace with the song, I could barely get a good look around the room. Something was going on. But what?

The music shifted once more, and again I found myself across from a new dance partner.

For a split second, I felt like my heart stopped beating.

The tall, well-built man standing across from me wearing a silver mask shaped like a wolf. And his eyes glimmered red.

I would have known him anywhere, but it was the tell-tale lock of blond hair hanging on his forehead and the smirk on his lips that gave him away.

Lionheart.

My whole body trembled, and to my surprise, tears welled in my eyes.

The musicians struck a cord, and we stepped toward one another. My knees shaking, I suddenly wondered if I needed to sit down.

"Now, Agent Louvel, don't get emotional," Lionheart whispered as he set his hand on mine. Rather than letting our hands lightly touch, he wrapped his fingers around mine.

"I... What are you—"

"I told you I wanted to see you in this dress. I must say, I haven't seen a lovelier sight in all my years."

"All of them? Well, that is impressive," I replied with a grin, gathering my wits about me once more.

We separated then, switching partners, but I kept my eyes on that old werewolf every moment. And he never looked away from me either. I could barely hear the music over the sound of my heartbeat. I waited impatiently for partners to switch so I could return to Lionheart once more.

"How did you know I was here?" I asked when we paired again once more.

"I inquired as to your whereabouts."

"Then decided to crash the party?"

"Crash is such an indelicate term. I wanted to see you. And I didn't want to wait."

"When did you get back?"

"Not long after you came here."

"You won't be leaving again. You'll be staying in London, right?"

Please say yes. Please say yes.

"I won't be leaving again," he said, his eyes lingering on my face. "I like your mask."

"Do you?"

Lionheart stepped close to me. He set his hand on my waist and pulled me close. In that single moment, the noise in the room seemed to fade, and there was only him and me.

"The mask. The dress. The hair. That rosy smell. I adore everything about you, Clemeny Louvel," he whispered.

"Now who's getting emotional?" I asked shakily.

"I thought it was time to say it."

"And you needed to go to the Holy Land to sort that out, did you?"

"Yes."

"And are you sorted out?"

"Very. Which is why I'm back. But as you said, I was not invited *here*. I won't be staying, but you know where to find me."

"And just like that, you're gone again?"

"I said what I came to say. Saw what I wanted to see."

"And?"

"And I was right. Red is your color."

The music chimed once more, indicating the line would move, and I would lose Lionheart in the shuffle.

"Richard," I whispered.

"I'll see you back in London," he said then gently touched my cheek. Stepping back, he slipped into the crowd then disappeared.

My knees shaking, I moved back in line with the other dancers, twisting and turning until I found myself across from Edwin once more.

He grinned at me, a nervous expression, on his face.

We twirled around one another once more. But I was preoccupied. I searched for Lionheart but didn't see him anywhere. More than that, the strange sense of the preternatural I'd been feeling all night was gone. It had been Lionheart I was sensing.

A moment later, the song concluded.

"Clemeny?" Edwin said, gently taking my arm. I could tell by the tone in his voice that it wasn't the first time he'd said my name.

"Sorry. I was preoccupied."

"It's okay. It's loud in here," he said then motioned for me to come with him. As we passed a servant, Edwin lifted two flutes of champagne and motioned for me to join him as we headed to the veranda outside.

I cast a glance over my shoulder. I looked for Lionheart, my mooneye working hard to pick up his shape, but I didn't see him anywhere.

Edwin handed me a flute of champagne then sipped from his glass. "Well, the setting is cooperating. It fits the ball," Edwin said, motioning to the mist-filled gardens and its silent statues. "It's supposed to rain tomorrow night though."

Was he talking about the weather?

"Lord Cabell installed clockwork gargoyles to keep watch on the grounds. I hope he remembered to deactivate them," I said, doing everything I could to get my mind off Lionheart. I drank my champagne, polishing off half the glass in one go.

Edwin nodded. "That sounds eccentric enough for him." Noticing my glass was empty, he took it from me then finished his own. Gesturing for me to wait a moment, he stepped back inside.

I turned and looked out at the garden, gripping the stone rail on the terrace. My heart was slamming in my chest. I breathed in deeply, trying to steady myself.

He was back.

He'd come back.

Thank God, he'd come back.

And he'd come to see me.

He'd come to…to say those things to me.

"I think the dance made us parched," Edwin said, returning once more with full glasses.

I took a deep breath, turned, then smiled at him.

Edwin raised an eyebrow at me. "Clemeny? You seem…distracted."

"It's nothing."

"I hope Lady Chadwick didn't upset you."

She had, but that wasn't what I was worried about. "It's all right. I understand."

"She will get used to you over time. She's actually a very kind woman. She just likes things to be done the way they have always been done. It escapes her notice that the world is changing…"

He was back.

He was sorted out.

"…In fact, I am glad she was able to meet you. It's

important that what little family I have gets to know you. With my father abroad..."

He's come to see me right away.

What had he said, 'I adore everything about you, Clemeny Louvel.'

"...and with Willowbrook Park in use by the Pellinores, my home and work is in London..."

But what did he mean he was sorted out? Had he had gone to the Holy Land to sort out his feeling for me? Was that what he said? He was settled on his feelings for me.

Did Lionheart actually love me?

Did I love him?

I did.

I loved him.

"...which is why I want to ask," Edwin said, then took my hand, startling me from my thoughts. He set our drinks aside, and to my immense surprise, bent on one knee. Edwin pulled off his mask and looked up at me, an earnest expression on his face.

"Edwin?"

Edwin cleared his throat then beamed a nervous smile at me. "Clemeny, you know how I feel about you. I love you. I was wondering... I was wondering if you would do me the honor of being my wife?"

CHAPTER 27
Rattled

I parked the steambike just outside the gate of Vesta's Grotto. Unlatching my cases, I grabbed my bags then turned and headed inside. The wrought iron gate squeaked when I entered. As I crossed the space, a soft autumn wind blew. Red and orange leaves danced across the path in front of me. Grand-mère's garden had faded with the coming of autumn, but her bright purple and gold chrysanthemums provided bright spots. I was surprised to see even a few late roses were still in bloom.

As I approached the house, I could hear Grand-mère talking to someone inside.

My emotions in a tumble, I was feeling entirely upside down. Even the energy at the Grotto set me on edge. Everywhere I went, I felt spirits. But All Hallows was always like this. Everything was awake.

I unlocked the door and entered the foyer, setting my cases down when I entered. The moment I did so, however, I was stricken with a strong sense of the preternatural.

Unless.

Grand-mère laughed lightly. "More tea?" she asked with a sweet chirp—a sound she reserved for visitors or attractive men.

"No, thank you," a husky male voice replied.

I suppressed a gasp then dashed into the parlor to find Grand-mère sitting across from Lionheart.

Hell's bells.

They both rose.

"Clemeny, oranges and lemons, I didn't even hear you come in," Grand-mère said.

"Well, we don't *all* have big ears," I said, raising a questioning eyebrow at Lionheart.

Grand-mère narrowed her eyes and looked at the bundle strapped to my chest. "What is that?"

Grinning, I fished out the little passenger and gently set the fluffy black bundle in Grand-mère's arms.

"A kitten?" Grand-mère practically squealed. "You brought me a kitten! Look at you, black as midnight," she told the sleepy kitten, scratching its head. She turned back to me. "Wherever did you find it?"

"I liberated it, so to speak."

"Oh my," Grand-mère said then turned to Lionheart.

"Clemeny, Professor Spencer stopped in to see you. He thought you might be back in London today. I told him I wasn't sure, but here you are."

"I caught an airship early this morning," I said, turning to Lionheart.

"You see," Grand-mère told him. "Well, let me leave you," she said, moving to go.

"Please," Lionheart said, motioning for her to stay. "Agent Louvel, may I have a word with you—outside?"

Remembering that the grotto was holy ground, and likely very painful for him—though he was hiding it well—I nodded. "Of course."

"It was a pleasure to meet you, Madame Louvel," Lionheart told Grand-mère.

"And you," she said, offering him a bright smile. "Come any time."

When Lionheart turned to go, Grand-mère caught my eye and gave me an approving nod.

Oh, good lord.

Lionheart and I headed outside.

"Is it better out here?" I asked.

He nodded. "Thank you. Your Grand-mère is delightful, but it felt like my blood was boiling in its veins."

The morning sunlight reflected on Lionheart's hair, capturing tones of gold and copper. His blue eyes shimmered brightly.

We walked toward the gate.

"Your bike is just there," I said, gesturing.

"I'm not here for the bike."

I paused. "Why are you here?"

"For you. I... I have been alive a very long time. I have never let myself love anyone out of fear. Bryony cared for me, and she paid the price. Her blood is on my hands, and it plagues me still. God made me like this, Clemeny. He made me and my brothers like this. The others have made peace with what we are, but it never sat right with me. You know I was married once, but she was my family's choosing. I cared for her, and I loved my son. But I... I've never really loved anyone. Never. Until you."

"Richard."

"Please, hear me out. It's taking everything I have to get through this."

I nodded.

"I went back to the beginning, back to the Holy Land, sought the word of God. Why was I granted this life? Why? Then I realized, if I had not lived this long, I never would have met Clemeny Louvel. I have been afraid all this time, afraid to love someone. I kept Bryony away, but she died anyway. I've been afraid to let myself love. I don't want anyone to get hurt. But then I realized, I've never met anyone stronger than you. Nothing can touch you. It's safe for me to love you, and I do. I love you, Clemeny. And I think you love me too."

I stared at him. My heart beat wildly in my chest. I couldn't catch a breath to speak.

"I know I can't offer you a normal life, but I am wise enough to know when I have met my match. You know what I am, and I am all yours, if you will have me."

I stared into his eyes. My mind reeled.

"Clemeny?"

"Edwin proposed," I blurted out, unable to form any kind of explanation that would make sense.

Lionheart's joyous, hopeful expression flattened at once. The light dimmed from his eyes, and he looked away. His hand trembling, he pushed back that stray lock of hair.

"Very well," he said. "We shall be brothers in arms as we have been which is well and I think I should go now but you should keep the bike," he muttered as he turned and walked away from me.

My hands shook.

Lionheart opened the gate, the metal squeaking.

Forcing my feet to move, I rushed after him.

"I said no," I called.

Lionheart stopped.

"I said no," I repeated as I met him on the sidewalk outside.

He turned and looked back at me. "You said no."

I nodded. "I said no."

Lionheart swallowed hard, covering his mouth with his hand as he regained his composure. Pulling himself back together—*were those actual tears in his eyes?*—he beamed a smile at me then turned toward the steambike.

"Do you like it?" he asked.

I nodded. "It got me where I needed to go."

"Chasing thieves, from what I hear."

"Not that the Templars were any help, but yes."

"Blackwood tells me there was an incident in the Dark District. Some thugs—wolves, of course—came in on an airship and were stirring up trouble."

"Sounds like they need to be taught a lesson."

"That they do. Shall we?" he asked, motioning to the bike.

"Why don't I drive?" I asked.

Lionheart chuckled. "I *am* the alpha."

"So am I."

Lionheart grinned.

I rolled my eyes. "Fine, I'll let you drive. Just this once."

Lionheart slipped on the steambike. I slid on behind him and wrapped my arms around him. I inhaled deeply, taking in his sharp, masculine scent. I allowed him to fill my senses. Maybe Lionheart got to drive, but this was the only reason I'd said yes. I pressed my cheek on his back and closed my eyes.

"Why, Agent Louvel. I do believe you missed me."

"More than you can ever imagine."

He paused then set his hand on mine. "I promise, you won't be sorry."

"Of course not. I carry two pistols loaded with silver bullets. Things can only go my way."

"Indeed? Then why did you let me drive?"

"Because I was overdue for a little rattling about."

"Oh, Agent Louvel. You haven't seen anything yet."

READ THE EXCITING CONCLUSION TO CLEMENY'S TALE IN
LYCANS AND LEGENDS

About the Author

New York Times and *USA Today* bestselling author Melanie Karsak is the author of *The Celtic Blood Series, The Road to Valhalla Series, The Celtic Rebels Series, Steampunk Fairy Tales* and many more works of fiction. The author currently lives in Florida with her husband and two children.

- amazon.com/author/melaniekarsak
- facebook.com/authormelaniekarsak
- instagram.com/karsakmelanie
- pinterest.com/melaniekarsak
- bookbub.com/authors/melanie-karsak
- youtube.com/@authormelaniekarsak

Also by Melanie Karsak

THE CELTIC BLOOD SERIES:

Highland Raven

Highland Blood

Highland Vengeance

Highland Queen

THE CELTIC REBELS SERIES:

Queen of Oak: A Novel of Boudica

Queen of Stone: A Novel of Boudica

Queen of Ash and Iron: A Novel of Boudica

THE ROAD TO VALHALLA SERIES:

Under the Strawberry Moon

Shield-Maiden: Under the Howling Moon

Shield-Maiden: Under the Hunter's Moon

Shield-Maiden: Under the Thunder Moon

Shield-Maiden: Under the Blood Moon

Shield-Maiden: Under the Dark Moon

THE SHADOWS OF VALHALLA SERIES:

Shield-Maiden: Winternights Gambit

Shield-Maiden: Gambit of Blood

Shield-Maiden: Gambit of Shadows

Shield-Maiden: Gambit of Swords

Eagles and Crows

The Blackthorn Queen

The Crow Queen

THE HARVESTING SERIES:

The Harvesting

Midway

The Shadow Aspect

Witch Wood

The Torn World

STEAMPUNK FAIRY TALES:

Curiouser and Curiouser: Steampunk Alice in Wonderland

Ice and Embers: Steampunk Snow Queen

Beauty and Beastly: Steampunk Beauty and the Beast

Golden Braids and Dragon Blades: Steampunk Rapunzel

THE RED CAPE SOCIETY

Wolves and Daggers

Alphas and Airships

Peppermint and Pentacles

Bitches and Brawlers

Howls and Hallows

Lycans and Legends

THE AIRSHIP RACING CHRONICLES:

Chasing the Star Garden

Chasing the Green Fairy

Chasing Christmas Past

THE CHANCELLOR FAIRY TALES:

The Glass Mermaid

The Cupcake Witch

The Fairy Godfather

The Vintage Medium

The Book Witch

Find these books and more on Amazon!

Printed in Great Britain
by Amazon